FORBIDDEN FRUIT

SELECTED TALES IN VERSE

JEAN DE LA FONTAINE, born in 1621 at Château-Thierry, north-east of Paris, was the eldest of the group of four illustrious poets associated with the reign of Louis XIV. He was also the slowest in maturing his poetic gift: when the first book of his *Contes et nouvelles en vers* appeared at the beginning of 1665, Molière, Racine and Boileau were all to varying degrees established writers. For most of his productive life, from 1665 to 1691, he continued to add to his series of *Contes*. His first book of *Fables* appeared in 1668 and continued, with the *Contes*, to be issued over an extended period, till 1694. Whereas the *Fables* won him friends from the start, the *Contes*, owing to their scabrous nature, procured him a load of trouble: not only was he twice blackballed for the French Academy, to which he finally gained election in 1683, but he had a few difficulties with the police as well. (Like his great predecessor and inspirer Boccaccio, he is said to have on his deathbed repented these follies of his youth.) Evidently a bachelor by temperament, La Fontaine was married off fairly promptly and had a son, but ceased cohabiting with his wife after a discreet interval – he found refuge in the households of a succession of princely protectors. He died in 1695.

GUIDO WALDMAN (born Lausanne, 1932, of American parents) devotes his days to working with authors and translators as a publisher's editor. He has been a translator himself since 1963, mostly of the Italian classics; these include Fogazzaro's *Piccolo Mondo Antico* (*A House Divided*), Ariosto's *Orlando Furioso* in a prose translation, and Boccaccio's *Decameron* (these two latter both published by Oxford University Press). He was editor and part-translator of *The Penguin Book of Italian Short Stories*. Alessandro Baricco's *Silk* is his most recent translation.

D1227510

JEAN DE LA FONTAINE

FORBIDDEN FRUIT

SELECTED TALES IN VERSE

Translated by Guido Waldman
Illustrated by Richard Shirley Smith

THE HARVILL PRESS
LONDON

This translation first published in 1998
by The Harvill Press,
84 Thornhill Road,
London N1 1RD

www.harvill-press.com

1 3 5 7 9 8 6 4 2

A CIP catalogue record for this book is available from the British Library

ISBN 1 86046 491 2 (hbk)
ISBN 1 86046 438 6 (pbk)

Designed and typeset in Fournier
at Libanus Press, Marlborough, Wiltshire

Printed and bound in Great Britain by Butler & Tanner Ltd
at Selwood Printing, Burgess Hill

Quand les gallants sont défendus,
C'est alors que l'on les souhaite.

LA FONTAINE, La Coupe enchantée

Translator's Note

In his Preface to the first edition of Book I, the author observes that his wish "has been to establish which approach is best suited to putting tales into verse: it has been his belief that verse-lines of irregular length partake of the feeling of prose, and that this approach, being the more natural one, is the best." Let the reader judge, he adds, whether the system works. I offer no apology for attempting to put into English a work known in this country, it would seem, only to scholars, so much have the *Fables* eclipsed this earlier work of La Fontaine; but the adoption of Ogden Nash's loose-limbed, conversational, *sui generis* prosody as the best vehicle for an English equivalent may need defending – and what La Fontaine wrote, as quoted above, would seem the best justification. The defining characteristics of the *Contes et nouvelles en vers* are, it seems to me, an infectious delight in the business of storytelling and a mischievous sense of fun, both in the author's constant urge to shove in his oar and in his playfulness with language and metre. In my own verbal tomfoolery I have sought to preserve what comes through so clearly in the originals – the author's easy complicity with his readers in teasing the maximum comic effect out of the situation he is recounting. Anarchic this Ogden Nashery may be, but I have sought nonetheless to observe two rules. The first is to use no word that has not conveyed its particular sense in English for at least the last hundred years. The second is to determine rhymes by reference to the ear rather than to the eye – albeit this has occasionally involved me in some freshly minted coinage which, although recognisable, has so far eluded the attention of the lexicographers.

Translating these absurdly under-valued verse tales, which in the original attest La Fontaine's technical skill every whit as much as his much translated *Fables*, has afforded the translator a great deal of amusement, which he hopes this volume – a small selection from the complete edition – will enable him to share.

G.W.

Contents

Joconde

In Lombardy there once lived a king so handsome he quite outdid Narcissus;
And at his court they were all madly jealous of him if they were a mister,
    and madly in love with him if they were a missus.
Now, one day as he was looking in his glass
He said: "I'm going to lay a bet
That for sheer seductiveness there's not a mortal to match me,
    let alone surpass,
And the best of my provinces is the stake I'm willing to set.
Moreover, if such a one exists, he has my word as a royal
That he'll receive such fair treatment from me he'll have no cause to be
    disloyal."
This consideration
Caused a Roman gentleman to step forward with the following
    observation:
"Sire," said he, "if beauty is that which arouses your curiosity,
Send for my brother, a man who may assuredly hold his own
Against all comers. I fancy myself here a bit of an expert, be it said
    without pomposity.
However, should you think that in this opinion I stand alone,
Should you dismiss me as a prey to self-deception,
Take not my word, but let judgment by these ladies be expressed.
He shall, if you will join me in this conception,
Relieve you of the task of assuaging so many throbbing hearts: you attend
    to some, he'll see to the rest.
So huge a gift of love laid at your feet must surely be importunate;
Dividing the task with a confederate may prove singularly fortunate."

"What you say," replied Astolfo (to give the Lombard king his name)
"Leaves me itching to meet your brother. Let him at once be sent for.
We'll see if our resident beauties will all rush to lay on him their claim,
And whether he's the man that the veriest prude is willing to relent for.
These discriminating ladies will, as you say, know best
How to apply the acid test."

Off went the gentleman to seek out Joconde, his sibling,
Who lived far from the madding crowd, amid meadows where the sheep
    would be a-nibbling.
A newly married man. Happy? To know the answer is more than I can claim –
His wife, to tell you the truth,
Was dainty, beautiful, and radiant with the bloom of youth,
So if he were not happy he'd have none but himself to blame.
His brother, then, arrived and instantly conveyed
The king's message. And found Joconde quite easy to persuade.
The friendship of a powerful sovereign who was also quite a charmer
Was not without its attraction for a gentleman who was, in a manner of
    speaking, but a farmer.
Add to which, it allowed his delectable consort to play the forsaken young
    widow to the hilt:
As she bade him farewell, copious tears were spilt.
"Alas," said she, "how can you leave me?
How can you be so hard of heart?
Ah, you are willing to bereave me
And spurn my constant love for such favours as the court may be ready
    to impart.
When you obtain them, you flatter yourself at your life's sudden
    enhancement,
Only to find the next day you've had to forfeit your advancement.
If your trouble is you're beginning to find me unexciting,
Just think how you've always found these peaceful pastures so inviting –
Why, whenever you've felt like a little nap,
There's always been a babbling brook to lull you off with your head
    upon my lap.
Oh these bosky copses, these rollicking rills –
Have you not found them hitherto the cure for all your ills?

And then there's me of course, to which you evidently attach not a great
    deal of weight:
Besides, it's now too late.
All right, so the only thing you can do is stand there and snigger;
Then off you go to court, where you'll cut such a dapper figure.
Me? I tell you, I expect to have joined the shades
Before the daylight fades."

History does not relate how Joconde was able to depart,
What steps he took, what answer 'twas he made:
And that which History passes over in silence is not something I would
    hazard to impart;
Let us merely observe that grief robbed him of speech, and there's no
    more to be said.
(Well, it's a neat suggestion
To avoid an awkward question.)
Seeing that he was about to take his leave and was not to be prevented,
His lady smothered him in kisses and, to cap it all, presented
Him with a darling little bracelet for his wrist.
"Don't lose it," she said. "You're to wear it night and day, I do insist,
To remind you that my love for you is passionate.
I spun it myself: out of my own tresses did I fashion it.
And depending from it you will duly
Find a portrait of yours truly."

You, gentle reader, are entitled to nurse the supposition
That the distraught lady would within the hour have given up
    the ghost.
But I, who enjoy a certain acquaintance with the fair sex, or so I like
    to boast,
I should not rush into assuming that her ill was past remission.
Off went Joconde but, don't ask me why or how,
He left the bracelet and painting behind,
(No doubt this was sheer absence of mind)
And that same morning galloped back as fast as his burdened
    steed would allow,
Cudgelling his brains the while for some excuse to avoid a nasty row.

Into the house he slipped, alone and unobserved,
Stole up to his chamber, and was not a little unnerved
To espy his wife on the bed with a lout of a groom gathered in her arms
And making the most of her charms.
Both slept and Joconde, feeling less than indulgent towards any ladies,
Was tempted to send the pair off to continue their sleep in Hades.
This instinct, however, is one that he did not pursue,
And, if you ask my opinion, that was the correct thing not to do:
The safest course to take in such a juncture
Is to keep the matter quiet as can be.
So he forbore to draw his dagger and puncture
Either sleeper: maybe 'twas caution played its part, or clemency.
On no account was he to wake this sleeping pair,
Else he'd have been in honour bound to take their lives.
"Live, then," said he, "most infamous of wives,
And if you die of sheer remorse, that'll be your affair."

Whereupon Joconde resumed his journey, brooding the whole way on
    what had befallen,
And every so often he would cry out in his affliction:
"Now, had it been a well built youth, maybe a tall 'un,
That might at least attenuate her dereliction.
But a groom reeking of the stable:
To swallow such a slight is more than I am able –
The more I think about it, the more I am inclined
To gnash my teeth. I mean, Love simply must be blind
To have perpetrated such a criminal mismatch:
Either that, or he is wickedly unkind;
Maybe these are the little plots this joker likes to hatch.
Or did he do it for a dare?
I'd not put it past him, I fear."

All this brooding on the enormity of which he had been victim
Quite served to spoil Jocondo's looks, so deeply did the thought of it
    afflict him.
Joconde: the answer to a maiden's prayer?
Cupid in person, of copious love-darts the conveyor?

When he arrived at court, what the ladies all said was: "My stars,
    if *this* is
Our promised heart-throb, our newly resident Narcissus,
All *I* can say is, the poor fellow's got the ague,
And I intend to avoid him like the plague.
Why all this palaver to fetch in a boy who's clearly overdone the dieting?
Frankly I find it more than a little disquieting."
Astolfo was cock-a-hoop, the brother exceedingly embarrassed,
For he had no idea why Joconde had turned up looking quite so harassed:
What was eating
The lad was something he was not going to go round repeating.
But despite his sunken cheeks and pasty complexion,
The latent elegance of his features was by no means beyond detection.
A little more convexity, a dash of sparkle in the eye,
And he might cease to be a leper by and by.
Eventually Love felt a touch of remorse – unless it was a touch of pique
That this moping fellow was putting off so many of his votaries:
Here was Joconde, the supposed idol of the lovesick coteries
Wasting away the flower of his youth when by all the rules he should have
    been all that was glossy and sleek.
So redemption finally came from the very source
That had hitherto knocked him so completely off course.
One day he happened to find himself all alone in a secret gallery, quite
    off the beaten track,
And heard a voice coming through what could have been only a thin
    partition wall.
Now this is what he heard: "My darling Kurti, this just won't do at all:
When I love you as much as I do it's quite wrong for you to be turning
    your back.
All right, I may be a little vain –
But there's no way you can find me plain.
My boy, I have suitors galore
Lining up to knock at my door
But you just stand there, as if you don't even know what I'm for!
Clearly you're happier playing cribbage with the pages
Though you know perfectly well I've been cooling my heels in this
    closet for ages.

Well? Doris brought you my convocation,
And you showered her with abuse, did you not? That was sheer
provocation!
You refused to throw in your hand until you'd made your pile
Without the least thought about *me*: come, don't even attempt
a denial."

Now Joconde's a man you could have knocked over with a feather
When he discovered who it was who were in there together.
Even if I gave you till tomorrow you'd never have guessed
Who the woman was who had thus expressed
Her feelings, nor who was the other person (and what his rank
and station)
Who was contributing nothing to the conversation.
All right, then: the complainant was the queen consort – you'd not
have got there, I warrant, in a semester;
And the indicted party was the court jester.
To have a view of them Joconde did not have to tax
His ingenuity: the wall was fairly riddled with cracks.
Well, Doris was the one who'd been selected
To make the lovers' confidential arrangements. She alone kept
possession of the closet's key;
But she dropped it, whereupon Joconde was the one who collected
It, as he observed to himself: "It won't be of as much use to her as it
will to me."
And indeed its employment
Afforded him some moments of rare enjoyment,
For this is the view he took:
"I'm not the only one. And if so engaging a prince
Can be so readily forsook
In favour of a misshapen dwarf, perhaps I was wrong to wince
At being supplanted by a fellow who ranks on a level with my cook."
This thought served to restore his spirits, and with them his appeal;
If he had been comely before, now he was simply sublime.
See how the fair sex came crowding at his heel
Though, not so long ago, it was unwilling to waste on him a moment
of its time.

Oh but observe the rush to gain his favour;
The primmest of the whalebone corsets could be seen to waver.
As for Astolfo, now was his turn to lose many a trick;
Well, no harm there – the swarm around him had been plenty thick.

The continuation of this tale must, however, be deferred
While we go back to the point where Joconde had overheard
The queen. The thought of what he'd seen left the poor fellow in
　　something of a quandary –
I mean, it made him hesitant and pondery
Because, when you're dealing with a monarch, you have to mind your
　　p's and q's
And not rush to present him with the news:
Not to talk out of turn
Is one of the first things you learn,
Else, the way you are rewarded
Is not something to be applauded.
For King Astolfo, however, our Joconde had a degree of devotion
Which quite precluded the notion
Of leaving the poor man in the dark
About what his lady got up to by way of a lark.
Now you've no alternative but to beat about the bush when you're
　　dealing with a royal,
Unless you want to bring him prematurely to the boil.
To avoid reducing his listener too quickly to tears
Joconde had to start a quantity of hares.
He recited a whole list of kings and Caesars
Whose wives had at one time or another been displeasers,
For all that a monarch is better cushioned than most against such reversals
By the time he'd put his entire court, not to mention Fortune herself,
　　through a number of rehearsals.
"Mark you, these sovereigns, sire: they all took it upon the chin
And simply would not permit their spouses' misdemeanours to get under
　　their skin.
Now look at me: The day I set out in answer to your invitation
It was borne in on me that Cuckoldry is one of the gods to whom
　　Marriage makes libation."

He gave the king a full account of his humiliation,
After which he turned
To explain how His Majesty'd been spurned.

"I know you," said the king, "for a man of honour, one who wears his
    heart upon his sleeve,
But there's nothing like the witness of one's own eyes
When something is alleged that is so hard to believe:
Lead me to your closet, therefore, and let us catch them by surprise."
Thus it was that Astolfo saw with his eyes and heard with his ears
A scene that would have reduced a lesser man to tears.
For a moment he was stunned and ready to expire,
But very soon he pulled himself together:
For in any situation, however dire,
He was not the man to let himself be driven to the end of his tether.
"Our better halves," said he, "have done us in the eye.
No doubt about it, they've really put one over.
Very well, now it's our turn for, by Jove, a
Smart lesson that here's a game at which two can play is a lesson they
    have to be taught by and by.
This is what we'll do: we'll change our names,
I'll be your cousin and dismiss my suite,
Forgoing, too, my usual claims
To your obeisance. This will make the pursuit of our amours all the
    more discreet.
Our pleasure would be harder to pursue
Were it necessary for Us to be paid all the honours that We are due."
Joconde assented. "Now," said the other, "as the conquest of females
    will constitute the kernel
Of our project, we'll do well to pack among our effects a logbook,
    diary or journal
Wherein to list the names of all comers
Who to our charms may prove to be succumbers.
We'll enter them in order of rank.
And there's one thing on which you can bank:
There'll be no page left that is blank
By the time we've quit our native shores –

Even the most recalcitrant of matrons will have flung open to
    us her doors.
We're both of us well built, and neither of us is a dim bunny;
Add to which, we carry deep purses for our money.
Would it not strike you as distinctly funny
If our approaches met with a resistance?
Given the assets I've mentioned, and our special line in endearments,
    I'd anticipate but small need for persistence."

They packed their bags, therefore, and left, not omitting to bring their
    log or roster.
Fortune favoured their courting. Many is the lady who lost her
Heart to this pair – I cannot give you the full score,
But anything in a skirt was fair game, and that's for sure.
The beauties who attracted their attention
Were rewarded with almost any gift they cared to mention.
The *grandes dames* alone, whether they were wife of the mayor, the
    chancellor or the garrison colonel,
Would all be vying for a place in the journal.
Hearts deemed hitherto impregnable to assault
Ran up the white flag before the first shot was fired.
"Stay!" the hard-heads among you will be saying, "These are
    assertions to be taken with a pinch of salt:
Even the most accomplished rake knows that for a state-of-the-art
    seduction both time and patience are required."
You may be right, sirs, I really wouldn't know;
Don't look to me to step outside my brief.
Marks for plausibility are not mine to bestow.
Besides, Ariosto is, of course, fully deserving of belief.
If you're going to pull up the narrator at every turn
He'll never come to the end of his tale.
All I can promise you folk is that if I still have a lesson to learn
I'll endeavour to absorb it without fail.

When our gallants had enjoyed a taste
Of everything (much as a bee will sip from flower to flower),

The king observed: "I see no need for haste,
When susceptible hearts are being flung at us in an absolute shower.
Let us therefore draw rein;
Indeed, if you ask me, it's none too soon to stop in our tracks,
For in love as at the table – or so we are informed by the quacks –
Too unbalanced a diet may give one a pain.
Truth to say, I have a touch of indigestion,
Which is why here is my suggestion:
Let's find a love-object and the two of us share it.
Of course if you have an objection, I want to hear it."

"Agreed," said Joconde. "And I know the lady who'll suit us down
        to the ground:
She's a beauty, has all her wits about her; I tell you, she's a dream,
And her spouse is by far the leading citizen for miles around."
"I grant you," said the king, "but frankly I, at any rate, seem
To have had enough of the cream:
Now take the skirts off your milkmaid and you'll find as much
        to treasure
As beneath those of your ladies of leisure.
Besides, why set ourselves a difficult assignment?
Think of all those fits of temper, that studied rudeness,
All that volatility, the backbiting that masquerades as shrewdness
One has to put up with when courting a lady of refinement.
Those women all need handling with kid gloves
Whereas your milkmaids can be the gentlest of doves.
No need to bend over backwards to please them,
Or risk a clip on the ear if you tease them;
No need to take them to the gala ball . . .
Really they're no trouble at all.
Just feed them any old pap
And they drop into your lap.
Your milkmaids are folk who are pliable,
And all we need is to choose one who's reliable,
Preferably one who's still wet behind the ears:
That's my recipe for a love-life without tears."

"Let us take our innkeeper's daughter," the other suggested.
"She's quite intact, I have this well attested.
Indeed she is a virgin through and through,
And innocent? – Why, even her doll could teach her a trick or two!"
"The thought entered my mind," the king replied;
"We'll have a word with her this very day,
And thereupon the two of us shall decide
Who is to introduce her to the amorous fray,
(Always assuming that the answer she gives us is Yea).
I know the honour of the first fruits is overrated,
But one imagines that in these matters deference to one's liege
     is indicated . . .
At all events, pray allow yourself to be placated."
"If ceremonial rules were only our concern
You'd be entitled naturally to claim
The precedence, but, permit me to observe, we're playing
     a different game.
Let us draw lots to see who takes first turn.
Here are two straws."
Well, it wasn't long before these two models of sobriety
Were exchanging epithets that would be vetoed in polite society.
Moreover Joconde proved the victor under Chance's laws.

Now as the landlord's daughter came to their room that night
On some innocuous errand, our gallants considered that the moment
     was right
To put the little maiden through her paces:
They praised her beauty and strove to capture her good graces,
And finally flashed a precious ring before her eyes, albeit without
     persistence:
This trinket, however, put an end to her resistance.
The bargain struck, a little while later, when all the hostelry
     had retired,
She slipped into their room and took her place in bed between
     them.
What happened next was the very thing to which all three aspired.
Did they make hay? Why, you should have seen them –

Especially Joconde, who fancied he was the first to make an entry
(As if to that moment her treasure had been constantly guarded by
　　a sentry).
Well, I won't hold it against him. I mean, let's keep a sense of
　　perspective –
For when a woman, never mind how feather-brained, has set herself
　　an objective
She'll pull the wool over anybody's eyes, no matter if he's the world's
　　greatest detective.
Solomon says something about this somewhere, and he comes down
　　to us as a man of great sagacity
(Though to have placed a finger on the passage would have been outside
　　Joconde's capacity).
So Joconde was in clover,
Convinced that he'd put one over
On his liege as he taught his pupil a new range of skills
Widely accepted as the cure for most ills.
Teacher and pupil, then, were highly satisfied with their induction –
Only I have to make one observation:
A young fellow had made an earlier application
To give her a little instruction
In the art of seduction.

The following night, and indeed the night after, their employment
Was conducive to enjoyment.
But the young fellow aforementioned
Could not but notice that his beloved was no longer quite so well
　　intentioned.
To lend colour to his suspicions he engaged in a little spying,
Caught her in the act, and made an enormous scene, which she found
　　dreadfully trying.
To pacify him she promised without fail
That the moment the guests had departed
His own wishes in the matter of trysts would absolutely prevail,
And he would accept that she was by no means stony hearted.
"Well, fiddlesticks to that!" the youth replied;
"Guests or no guests, I'm having you tonight,

Or else I may decide
To spill the beans." This left the girl in something of a plight.
"What's to be done, then? They have my promise and I must not
 abuse it,
And, Heavens! I've *earned* that ring, and now you'll make me lose it."
"Nay, have no fear for your ring," the young man told her roundly,
"Just tell me this: Do both of them sleep soundly?"
"They do," said she. "But all night long I have to lie between them like
 pig in the middle.
And while I'm engaged with the one, the other, who's waiting to put
 in a bid'll
Often just turn over on his side
And softly into slumber glide,
Which leaves me with vacant possession
(To use their own expression)."
"I'll come to you, then, during their first sleep."
At this the poor girl was struck all of a heap:
"Pray don't do that, it would be too appalling!"
"Come. No need to worry. Now please stop your bawling –
And one thing more:
Remember not to lock the door."

She left it open, and in stole her friend,
Approached the foot of the bed,
Beneath the covers inserted his head,
And only God knows how he contrived to ascend
Her, and what came next, but the truth is, the two lovers who flanked
 her incurred the same illusion
And innocently drew the same conclusion.
They both awoke, perplexed by such a burst of activity.
"What's got into Joconde?" mused the king. "I know that towards
 amorous exercise he shares my proclivity,
But he's really taking more than his share,
And if it doesn't leave him knocked out, that will be most unfair."
Similar sentiments were, be it said, nurtured by Joconde.
Now when the young visitor, having recruited his strength,

Drew an additional ration for the next day and the day after and indeed for the
    rest of the week, at length,
The honoured guests having fallen asleep and a new day having dawned,
He slipped out by the same route by which he had made his entry.
The girl followed him out,
Being in some doubt
Whether she could cope with a further onslaught from her
    attendant gentry.

On their both awaking, the king addressed his friend:
"Pray, don't think of getting up after your night of strenuous exertion;
A period of complete rest must now, I insist, attend
Your wearied frame." "Now fancy! *Yours* was the frame that has all night
    suffered some rude coercion.
The remedy you propose is precisely what you stand in need of."
"Me!" the king exclaimed. "Now that's sheer nonsense that I'll not take
    heed of.
'Rude coercion' indeed! Here was I with saintly patience waiting
Until it was clear you were never going to be done with your mating –
Nay, you're a selfish brute, I'll be bound:
You were clearly intent on riding the poor lass into the ground,
And for no better reason than to drive me to distraction
By denying me *my* moment's satisfaction.
So what do you suppose?
I had no choice but to turn over and sink into a doze.
And yet I'd gladly have run with her a couple of laps
Were it not that your performance was seamless and innocent of gaps."
"All right, keep teasing, but I find your joke in not the best of taste.
I am your vassal, you've made that very clear.
Is it not enough that all night long you had the girl enlaced
In your arms? Very well. Do with her as you will for all *I* care:
We'll see how long it takes your fire to burn out." "I see myself burning
    with a lifelong flame
If we have another night when you deprive me of my claim."
"Enough, my lord, enough of this derision.
I've reached the point where I shall, by your leave, withdraw myself
    from your royal supervision."

This proposal left the king thoroughly nettled
– And left their quarrel even further from being settled –
Indeed things might have got completely out of hand
If the girl had not opportunely arrived at Astolfo's command.
They told her the reason for their fury
And appointed her both judge and jury.
She blushed for shame and on her knees she fell,
And clarified for them the entire mystery.
Now although a hideous penalty might well have emerged from this
    consistory,
The two gallants found her tale quite hilarious, and all was well.
She had her ring, and of silver coinage a handsome provision;
In short, to conclude this maiden's story with a degree of concision,
This served her as a dowry when, not long after, the nuptial knot was tied,
The day her father gave her away as an untarnished bride.

This brings our venturesome pair to the end of their adventures.
    They returned
Laden with prizes that had, I fear, been rather cheaply earned:
Their claim
To legendary fame
Cost them what? A little nimble footwork and a thick application of charm
Which earned them golden opinions, with very little risk of coming
    to harm.
Highly pleased with themselves at having swept so many ladies off their
    feet, and noticing, on enquiry,
That there was not a single blank space left within their diary,
The Lombard king said to his friend:
"Home by the shortest route I suggest we wend
Our way. If our wives are unfaithful, while we needn't condone,
We may at least take comfort, for they're clearly not alone.
The time may come when not even the lightest kiss
Will be accorded except within the confines of true wedded bliss.
But for that the planets will have to enter a new conjunction:
For the present it is evident that some perverse star is exercising its function.
Spouses today are the victims of sharp practice
And, moreover, the fact is

We are not masters of our every thought and action,
Not so long as there are sorcerers whose idea of satisfaction
Is to play fast and loose with people's marital vows
And cast spells over wedded couples to set them at sixes and sevens
And breed the most extravagant domestic rows.
Wait: Perhaps this is what they've done to my wife and yours!
    Good Heavens –
Supposing that both of us were seeing
Things that in fact were devoid of objective being!
Come, let us both return to the strait and narrow path
And resume our roles as pillars of the home and hearth.
Who knows? Absence, they say, makes the heart grow fonder:
Maybe our wives will each be glad to retrieve her dear absconder –
Or jealousy may restore to us the place in their hearts that was forfeit
    by familiarity."
And, as it turned out, between Astolfo's prediction and what ensued
    there was happily no disparity.

Home once more, our two adventurers were received with ready hospitality,
And if they were scolded too, this was only a formality.
They each were entitled to a generous allowance of kisses
From their respective missus,
And in making up for lost time the reunited couples were so sedulous
They would have left the rest of us incredulous.
Oh how they skipped and danced,
Frolicked and pranced,
And about the dwarf, not a word,
Nor about the groom – or so I have inferred.
Each husband clove religiously to his wife
To live in peace and friendship, as happy as could be, for the rest of
    his life.
The queen in the fulfilment of her duties now proved conscientious,
Nor could Joconde's dear wife be remotely called licentious,
Nor indeed could many another woman – the supply of virtuous ladies,
    let us conclude, is plenteous.

(Derived from Ariosto: *Orlando Furioso*, XXVIII, 4ff)

Cuckolded, Thrashed, Delighted

Not so long ago there was a young sprig who had paid
A largely unprofitable visit to Rome,
And was now on his way home.
Well, on his return journey he was content to dawdle, and to accept
    any excuse to be delayed,
Especially on occasions where his inn provided
Good wine, good quarters, and a pretty serving wench with whom
    his bed might be divided.
Stopping one day in a little town,
He noticed a lady attended by her page;
Fair of face, she was, dainty as well, and sporting an elegant gown –
One look was enough for him to gauge
That she was a quarry worth pursuing.
Well, our pilgrim had come away with indulgences by the sack,
But to call him a model of virtue would be inexac' –
That's the way of the world. Besides, a lady is worth the wooing
When she has an alluring disposition,
High spirits, dazzling beauty, and a look in her eye to send a man to
    his perdition.
In a word, she had it all
Except for a friend with whom to share it.
And the fact is, our lad was lost beyond recall –
He yearned for her so much he simply couldn't bear it.
The first thing he did therefore was to enquire
Who the lady was, and he was told she was the missus of the local squire.
"His nibs has but lately annexed her

As his married partner, for all that his head sports but four hairs, every
    one of them grey,
But if she has promised to love, cherish and obey,
That will be because he *is* the local nob – and the size of his estate will
    not have vexed her."

After taking good note of all he had been told
Our pilgrim conceived a solid expectation of striking gold,
And here is how he reckoned to proceed.
First he dismissed his pages to find their billet in the neighbouring
    borough;
Then up he went to the manor, spoke to its lord and said: "I'm the man
    you need:
I'm young and keen as mustard, can turn my hand to anything, and
    besides, am nothing if not thorough."
The squire found all of this highly satisfactory,
And appointed him master of the falcons –
Having first consulted his wife, who turned out to be not in the least
    refractory,
Indeed she persuaded him he'd not find a better one west of the Balkans.
You see, the falconer and the lady hit it off right from the start
And, being a lady-killer of some experience,
He wasted no time in offering her his heart.
Not that he'd set himself a simple task, design and execution being at
    a considerable variance:
The old man worshipped the ground trodden upon by his bride
And seldom left her side
Except when he was off with his hawks and hounds.
His falconer perforce had to go too, though he'd have been happier
    loitering within the grounds.
The lady held a similar inclination
But for the present all they could do was wait and watch the situation:
And if I venture that they found this delay a sore affliction
I believe I can do so without fear of contradiction.

Now Love, who had not remained indifferent to their plight,
Inspired the lady to speak thus to her husband one night:

"Of all your retinue which one in your service, do you feel,
Shows the greatest zeal?"
"Upon my word, I've always held the view
That my falconer is quite exceptionally good and true:
There we have a lad in whom I'll trust quite blindly."
"Don't think," said she, "I aim to speak unkindly
But, on the contrary, he's a man to view with some suspicion.
Why, only the other day he was making me an indecent proposition.
Heavens, was I shocked! I scarce believed my ears;
My first thought was to let fly with my nails, indeed to strangle
Him, until it occurred to me to approach this from a different angle,
For one prefers not to trumpet these affairs.
What's more, in case he should deny it,
I told him: 'If you want to, we could try it.
In the garden by the pear tree after dark
I'll meet you. But this,' I said, 'is what you have to mark:
My husband sticks to me like my shadow, not because he considers
    me suspectable
But because he loves me and finds me endlessly delectable.
The only time we're safe from his adoring
Is when he's gone to sleep and started snoring.
So that is when, his vigilance discardin',
I can slip out of bed and join you in the garden.'
That then, my friend,
Is whither matters tend."

At this the worthy squire
Found it impossible to conceal his ire,
But his lady said: "Gently does it, dear.
Why not catch him red-handed, then you can give him more than a clip
    over the ear!
By the pear tree, the first on the left as you enter the garden you'll find him.
Now, rather than simply creeping up behind him,
Here's what you do: You wear my skirts and turn up in disguise –
I mean stand in for me
And give yourself leisure to listen to his infamy
And credit thus the witness of *your* eyes.

You'll bring a stick. Apply it to his nether quarters
Until he drops, to teach him to keep his hands off honest burghers'
    daughters."
Her husband swallowed all of this hook, line and sinker –
He would not be rated the world's profoundest thinker.
I mean, a fellow may be the soul of kindness
And yet be not exempt from blindness.

When the moment came to catch the gallant, his employer,
Decked out in his wife's head-dress and billowing skirt,
Dashed away into the garden in a state of high alert,
To catch this blight infesting the domestic foyer.
But, I have to declare:
There was nobody there –
Which was not what he had been expecting.
And while he lingered out there, teeth chattering and perishing with cold,
Little did he realise that the wolf was already in the fold,
For after the lad had spent a while inspecting
The neighbourhood, he went to join his mistress in her bed.
When Love has taken a hand, so I've heard it said,
And the lady is more than willing, indeed all too inviting,
Then the love-play tends to prove not unexciting.
But the game, alas, could not be made to last for ever
Because their plan involved a further endeavour;
When their time was up
The lady sent him on his way (though not before offering him a stirrup cup).
Into the garden he ran, where his nibs, with growing dismay
And seething impatience cursed the man's delay.
Now when the lad spotted him he made a play
Of taking his master for his master's spouse
And shouted: "Monstrous woman! To play so mean a trick upon your lord
And bring such treachery within this noble house!
Is this for his unfailing kindness a merited reward?
Well you are, God be my witness, an utter disgrace:
Myself, I almost hesitated to come, for it passed belief
That you would truly have the face
To cause your husband such injury and grief.

You need a sweetheart, do you? But I'm not your man —
So if I fixed this meeting, that was simply in my plan
To test the mettle of your marriage vow,
For look, I don't say that I'm perfect, but to romp with you in bed
Is not a thought that's ever come into my head:
I have, thank God, some small concern for your house, so that's a thing
    it simply won't allow.
My word! The effrontery of this woman! She must be bold as brass ter
Think I'd ever practise such deceit upon my master!
No, you little hussy, I'm going to tan your hide,
Then tell my master what sort of a woman he's taken as his bride."
Our squire listened to all this with tears of joy
And murmured in his ecstasy: "Now *there*'s my boy!
Praise be to God, for truly I've been graced
With wife and servant both so good and chaste."
Nor was that all, for the lad produced a cudgel he'd concealed
And left the old man's shoulders badly raw and wealed
(Or was it rather a belting
That produced all that welting?)
At all events, he soundly flogged his master
To get him back indoors p'raps all the faster.

In truth the luckless squire could have wished that in his service the fellow
Had been just a shade more mellow.
Still, for his smarting skin it was great consolation
To remember this boy so charged with righteous indignation.
He found his wife in bed and told her all that had occurred:
"My honey, were we both to live another hundred years
We'll neither of us find ourselves a lad who is remotely to be preferred;
He is indeed a treasure to be valued above all his peers.
I mean to find him a wife here in this district. And I'm asking you to try
To hold him in the same affection as do I."
"Your wish, dear husband, will have my complete concurrence;
Pray count on it with the most serene assurance."

(Derived from Boccaccio: *The Decameron*, VII. 7)

The Cradle

There once was an innkeeper, not far from Rome,
On the road out to Florence;
He was no big noise – his was an 'umble 'ome,
And he didn't cater for the big spenders, in fact he held them in
    abhorrence.
If required to offer board *and* lodging,
That's something he would be dodging.
His wife had put barely thirty years behind her
And still was an appetising morsel, the way the Good Lord had
    designed her.
Which left a brace of youngsters to consider:
A boy of one, a girl of age to produce one for the likeliest bidder.

Enter now Pinuccio, young sprig, and well connected,
Who chanced upon her as he went his ways,
Gave her a glance, then came back and inspected
The creature and went off in an enraptured daze,
Finding in her all that is most charming,
Not to say disarming,
Doe-eyed and full of allurement –
He had to attend without a moment's delay to her procurement.
Well, the lad was not a mute, nor the lass hard of hearing,
So he told her where matters stood, and she found this rather cheering.
"What a pity,"
Said he, "that we can't get straight down to the nitty-gritty."

You see, to be hooked, avow it, and be listened to was all as one
For this young man, who was built like Apollo –
Winning her heart? It was already won.
"Just you lead off," said she, "and I will surely follow."
Besides, the girl would never give the time of day
To those who laboured to fetch in the hay;
Not that she thought herself cut out for a higher station
But, for all her tender years,
She had sufficient spirit – and indeed discrimination –
To decide her local suitors left her bored to tears.
So although many lads had sought her hand in marriage,
The maiden (called Colette)
Was only ever ready to disparage
The timid and give the cold shoulder
To the bolder,
And leave all her gallants to fume and to fret.
If she had a bee in her bonnet,
The name Pinuccio was clearly writ upon it.
Now lengthy tête-à-têtes were not permitted
And they found their wits against all manner of obstacles were pitted.
So if they were to fix a tryst in order to assuage their mutual passion,
What they'd be needing was a generous ration
Of miracles. Very well, this merely served to put them on their mettle:
Come, doting parents, take note of my advice,
Don't drive your children to the brink,
(This goes for spouses too, I am inclined to think)
For when Love grasps the challenge, you'll be left to settle
For paying out at an inflated price.

One evening, when the weather was distinctly grey,
Pinuccio turned up at this hostelry and asked if he might stay,
He and a mate.
"Why damn it, sir, you've left it rather late,"
Replied mine host. "Besides, we're pretty squeezed,
Just take a look, we're bulging to the rafters fit to burst.
Fact is, my wife and I would be quite pleased
If you would try a couple of other places first.

This berth is not for men of your condition."

"Come now," Pinuccio said, "you must have some shakedown left for
    disposition."

"All that we have, sir, is our bedroom and two beds:

One is for guests; the other's where we inmates lay our heads.

If you don't mind bedding down in company, your mate and you,

Well . . . very well, we'll see what we can do."

"Most gladly," said the gallant. "Now then, hurry up

And lay the table, for we want to sup."

They ate their dinner, then upstairs they went, the moment they were
    through.

Pinuccio made a note of exactly how the chamber was disposed

– As Colette had proposed –

And when all the other occupants had hit the hay

A truckle-bed was made up on which the girl might lay.

On one side of the door the genial host's bed stood;

On t'other the guests' bed had to go – there was no other place it could.

Between the two, the cradle of the babe so recently nascent,

But this was pulled across so that it stood adjacent

To his mother's bed. Now here's what set the cat among the pigeons,
    when our gallant's mate

Was to become the unwitting instrument of Fate.

'Twas midnight, and the landlord evidently slept;

His missus also slumbered,

Whereas Pinuccio, impatient man, counted off each minute – oh, how
    they seemed unnumbered! –

Until the magic moment, then he crept

Towards the truckle-bed. With careful, muffled steps he trod,

Approached, and found his loved one very wide awake

– Well of course: you'd not expect to find her in the land of Nod!

The gallant found her a fast learner, too, and no mistake;

He taught her games that I dare say leave one out of breath

But certainly never wearied to death.

If either called a truce, 'twas quickly broken:

These humours seldom flag once they are woken.

Now while this pair were going hell for leather
In the truckle-bed, Pinuccio's friend had to get up to answer
    Nature's call,
Reached for the door to pass into the hall,
Ran up against the cradle – it and the landlord's bed being pushed
    together –
Tugged it (with sleeping babe) discreetly to his side,
For he'd have made a noise trying to clear it in one stride.
On his return he sidled past the tot,
And never thought to relocate its cot;
Climbed into bed and started counting sheep
Until the Good Lord finally sent him sleep.
A little while later, something somewhere fell down with a thump,
Enough to make anybody jump.
Mother woke up, and shuffled out to make a quick investigation,
And, on her return, suffered an aberration:
She felt the cot, which no longer was annexed
To her husband's bed and "Holy Moses!" uttered she; "here I am in
    naught but my chemise
About to join these gentlemen in *their* bed, if you please!
I fear my husband would have been a trifle vexed.
Thank God I have the cradle here to guide me:
That way I know I have the right partner beside me."
This said, she hopped straight into bed
Beside the lad. Well, I don't have to tell you where *that* led,
For the boy was not slow-witted, nor sluggish his reaction,
And lost no time in giving satisfaction.
He addressed his task with gratifying agility
And fulfilled the husband's role with rare ability.
But no, I lie – in truth there are some things a man can overdo,
And, failing to remember that he was disguised,
Left Mother really quite surprised:
"My word," said she, "until this moment I never knew
Our better half could give us such a jolt –
The man's as active as a four-year colt.
Mark you, it must be said, I've no objection
If thus he wants to show me his affection."

These words were scarcely uttered when the lad with whom she lay
Showed himself more than ready to resume the fray.
The lady, as I've already once observed,
Was freshest produce, and very well preserved.

Meanwhile Colette was racked
By mounting fear that with the coming daylight she'd be rumbled
    in the act,
So she sent her Pinuccio back to his own bed –
But the boy got in with his host instead:
The reason for this aberration
Was that, of course, the crib was in its new location.
"I tell you, chum," said he,
With no attempt to moderate his voice
(When folk are pleased, they don't accord themselves the choice),
"I'd give a lot to find the words to share my glee
With you. It is a crying shame
You've had no chance to play my kind of game.
Colette, now: *there*'s a saucy one, upon my word!
Once you get her started, she's not easily deterred.
I've seen 'em in all shapes and sizes, but she's unique –
What a physique!
Skin like a babe's posterior
Waist? A wasp's is frankly inferior.
And what a chest!
Enough to make you almost overlook the rest.
So then, before we reached the finishing post
We'd run the course six times: six, that is no idle boast."

The landlord, half asleep, mumbled a mutterance –
The closest he could get to utterance.
His wife whispered into what she took to be her husband's ear:
"Now that's the last time you're to lodge this enterprising pair;
You must be deaf if you can't hear them. Listen!"
At this the host sat up and started hissin':
"Now what's the game they've come in here to play?
Well, hark at him – the fellow's got a nerve

To brag about his tumble in the hay!
Right, my fine popinjay, you'll get what you deserve.
If your idea is we bring up our fillies
For no better purpose than to exercise your w———s
I'll have you think again. Now out, sir, before you join the martyrs.
And you, my girl, I'll have your guts for garters."

These words indeed suggested a temper beginning to smoulder,
And Pinuccio's blood ran colder;
He couldn't find his pulse, he felt a creeping on his skin.
Nay, in the ensuing silence you could have heard the dropping of a pin.
Colette, believe me, could only lie there and quail,
While Mother, awake at last to just what had occurred,
Saw that she had the tiger by the tail.
Pinuccio's friend by now too had inferred
The cradle was the culprit all the while.
"Pinuccio," said he therefore with a smile,
"How many times, boy, have I had to tell you
Those jugs of wine are going to prove your ruin:
You crash about and talk in your sleep without the least idea what
      you are doin'
– Why, you even fancy you have gone a-wooin'!
No wonder folk decide they must expel you.
Come back to bed." Pinuccio caught the drift,
And having something of a Thespian gift
Went weaving, groping back across the floor.
Mine host was quite persuaded, that's for sure.
Now Mother too was ready to put in her oar:
She crossed the room and slid in with Colette;
Emboldened now that she was tucked up with her pet,
"You do surprise me, dear, upon my word,"
Said wife to husband, "I cannot think how that which you allege
      might have occurred,
How our Colette could have been slept with and deflowered:
All night long, you see, I've been with her embowered.
She has, my dear, been truly unapproachable,

29

Her conduct no worse than mine – and mine I trust you find quite
    irreproachable.
Our friend has pulled the wool over our eyes."
"Enough, enough," cried he. "To doubt you would perhaps be not
    altogether wise."
The sun was risen now and it was time to rise.
As they got up you might have caught
On certain faces something like a secret smile;
Secrets they had, but no, they were divulging naught –
Where would we be without a touch of guile?

(Derived from Boccaccio: *The Decameron*, IX.6)

Three Wives and Their Bet

One day three wives were chatting over a glass of wine or two,
And reminiscing about the tricks they'd got away with.
They each of them had a young man to play with,
While two of them were in full charge of their households, as was no less
    than their due.
The first one said: "My husband's a real paragon, there's not another in
    town to beat him:
I can take my pleasures whenever I like, it's so easy to cheat him,
The man is so receptive
To suggestion he's a total dim-wit, why, this log is more perceptive.
No need to make much effort: with just a little coaxing you'll be sure
He'll be persuaded that three and two make four."
"Well, Heavens!" said the second, "if he were mine I'd give the oaf away,
For the fact is, there's just no fun in making hay
If the sun never stops shining. No, give me a man who's always there to
    hinder –
What better way to set alight the tinder!
So be content to lead yours by the nose;
Me, if *I*'m to spend time with my beaux,
I have to play a crafty hand, to choose my time and place discreetly,
And if I'm to circumvent him I must do it oh so neatly.
Mark you, a life without a bit of sport –
Perish the thought!
It's all the merrier, too, when your lover's head over ears
In love. I'd not exchange husband or lover in a million years."

The third concluded the debate and in her peroration
Placated the two ladies by suggesting
That Cupid wholly favoured husbands who found their wives' leisure
    activities quite uninteresting,
But was not averse to those who charged their wives' *affaires* with
    complication.

This point settled, there followed much contention
As each was intent on giving her amorous triumphs an extensive
    mention,
When in stepped the third and said: "Come, enough of this loquacity.
If you really want to know which of us has the greatest capacity
For hoodwinking spouses, let us each devise right now some fresh
    invention.
There'll be a forfeit for the least successful schemer."
"Now that," said the other two in chorus, "would seem a
Very sound idea.
Moreover we all of us must swear
To make a true report, free of embellishment or omission,
Of what we did accomplish. As for a judge, let us make our submission
To you, Marisa." The task of judgment being thus happily conceded,
We shall now see how each of them proceeded.

The lady in our threesome whose life was the most constricted
Happened at this point to be amorously addicted
To a cherub of a boy, a beardless youth whose very femininity
Was to give the stratagem its measure of concinnity.
The luckless pair had never yet succeeded
In being together for as many minutes as were needed
To consummate their passion. They were perforce impeded
As they sought fresh opportunities, new places of assignation.
Now to put her new plan into operation
The lady dressed the boy in maid's attire.
The youth knocked at the door
And with downcast eyes, looking unspeakably demure,
Advised the master of the house that he was a chambermaid for hire.

The master looked her over and at once concluded that here was a gift
Of Fortune – a maid whose skirts he'd dearly love to lift.
Never, thought he, had he been offered such a charmer,
(Not that, where *he* was concerned, Cupid's darts had to pierce any
    great thickness of armour).
A pretty chambermaid and a husband inclined to lechery
Did require of the wife some pretence of reluctance, so she was not at
    once persuaded
Until her thwarted spouse taxed her with her treachery.
Those first days, however, the new maid did
Her best to evade the master, who feigned to look the other way
If she was in the room. There came, however, the day
When she'd been so enticed with gifts and promises that she pretended
    to be fired
With the urge to do as the master desired.
One evening she came to him with a message from her mistress,
    pleading
Indisposition, and requiring to sleep in her own room as being the most
    salutary proceeding.
Thereupon, maid and master, by common (if partly feigned) consent
    prepared for bed.
Now, with the man recumbent and the maid stepping out of her skirt –
    her cap still on her head –
Who should walk in but Madam? And who was it who was put
In an awkward situation, with the boot on the wrong foot?
"Well now," said she with a merry laugh, "would I be right in
    surmising
That Our normal diet is no longer sufficiently appetising
For Our jaded palate? Ah, what a shame that hitherto you've never
    hinted . . .
I'd have seen to engaging our maids young and tender and newly
    minted.
Now for a reason I can't go into I have to say I'm sorry –
This maid is unavailable, you'll have to seek a different quarry.
And as for you, you common little tart
Of a chambermaid with your highfalutin ideas –
Clearly you want to dine out of the same dish as me, as if that's smart!

Well, what do *I* care? If I'm to eat from a different dish, that's no cause
    for tears:
There are plenty of others just as well made
And I, thank God, have all that it takes
To continue attracting the rakes,
So my ejection into the street can assuredly be delayed.
Enough of that. I have a good solution, no need to repine:
From this night on, you'll lie in no other bed but mine!
Come, does this not seem to have impressed her?
Quick, off we go. The bed in which I sleep's the only place to nest her.
You can come back in the morning to retrieve
Your things. Indeed I'd toss you out of doors just as you are, but
    I believe
That shame and scandal would be best averted
And we'd prefer to leave the neighbours unalerted.
Besides, I'm a kind soul and ready to make light of this transgression,
Indeed, you will obtain from me a fair report
Now that I've no reason for disquiet, for I fancy I may abort
Your every stratagem; you'll stick to me night and day, like my
    shadow, if that's the right expression."
Hearing these words the servant made to hang her head,
Induced a tear or two, picked up her things and fled
The room, without a word nor any need for further objurgations.
Now she was to play a second role, fulfilling in the household two
    separate occupations –
Squire by night and parlourmaid by day,
Thus satisfying two domestic needs as best she may.
As for the luckless husband, he had to count himself fortunate
To escape scot free from a wife who tended to be importunate.
And as he slumbered in his lonesome bed, the lovers had abundant
    leisure
To pursue their amorous pleasure.
Furthermore, being so much of the same persuasion,
They gathered ye rosebuds on every conceivable occasion.
Thus it was that the husband's amours did not turn out as planned
And the wife obtained the upper hand.

The second wife had less call to be sedulous
In hoodwinking her spouse, for he was all too credulous.
All it took was a pear tree beneath which she sat with her husband when, as
    you shall hear,
She felt a sudden craving for a pear.
Now there stood her footman, a strapping lad, well spoken and endowed
    with presence
– A far cry from any of your peasants –
And just the man to keep order below stairs.
"I wouldn't mind trying one of those pears,"
She said; "so up you climb, William, and shake us down a few."
Once up the tree, the man put on a show of scandal and disgust,
As if he'd found the couple making love. "Come, really sir, come,
    this will never do!"
He cried. "By all means mount your lady if you must,
But not right here with servants looking on.
While I'd not dream of course of criticising
I have to say I find it most surprising
That you just couldn't wait till I was gone.
All right, a mere footman counts for little, I expect
Is what you feel – but don't you owe yourselves that much respect?
What has come over you? Can you not suffer but a small adjournment?
When such intimacies are deferred
– You may take it from any person of discernment –
They breed the more excitement. Besides, pray rest assured,
These summer nights are still sufficiently protracted
To allow for sexual congress to be suitably enacted.
And why out here? Possessed as you are of so many bedrooms, such
    nice beds
Wherein to disport yourselves and to behave like newly-weds."
"What is he going on about?" the wife enquired.
"The fellow must be dreaming. Love-play? I cannot claim to catch his drift.
Come down, my friend, come, shift
Your weight out of that tree, for nought else is desired."
The man descended. "Well," his master asked, "is love-play now
    proceeding?"

WILLIAM: Not now.

HUSBAND: Not *now*?

WILLIAM: Not at this moment – that much I'm conceding.
I am willing, though, to be skinned alive if, but this moment past,
You and your lady's antics were not such as to leave your servant
    quite aghast.

WIFE: Come, stop it, man! Enough now of your lip!
That kind of talk is asking for the whip.

HUSBAND: No, no, my dear. When we're dealing with fools, permit me
    to know what I am doing.

WILLIAM: What is foolish about a man who views what he is viewing?

WIFE: Well? What is it you saw?

WILLIAM: I saw the Master and yourself, the one to the other hitched –
Unless of course this pear tree is bewitched.

WIFE: Bewitched? Fiddlesticks!

HUSBAND: Now this I have to see.
I'm climbing up – we'll know the truth once I've gone up the tree.

The moment the husband had begun to climb,
The wife and footman wasted little time
Before becoming locked in passionate embraces.
Observing this, the husband gave a yell and, as happens in such cases,
Dropped from the tree so fast he almost broke his clavicle,
(And yet not fast enough to be preventing
His honour from receiving quite a denting).
"Stop! Stop!" he cried. "This conduct's too depravical!
Hey! What! My Heavens! Before my very eyes!"

WIFE: Come, dearest, do acquaint us with the meaning of
    these cries.

HUSBAND: You dare to ask?

WIFE: Why not?

HUSBAND: Am I not within my rights
To accuse you of this effrontery?

WIFE: Dear me, I have to say these flights
Of oratory leave one bewildered.

HUSBAND: Are you proposing to deny
That this young attendant was just now attending to your thigh?

WIFE: You must be dreaming.

HUSBAND: Then what's the explanation?
Is it my sight that's gone, or is it my cerebration?

WIFE: Do you consider me to be so depleted of any sense of fitness
As to do such a thing while you stand by as witness?
And would I not find sufficient hours in the day
At whatever moment I was in a mood to play?

HUSBAND: Well, I don't know what to say. It could be that our tree
Is playing us tricks. I'll try again and see.

The instant he was up swaying amid the boughs
William resumed his efforts; but this time the spouse
Viewed the whole thing quite equably, returned to the ground with
    care, and "All is well,"
Said he, "let's look no further – the tree's under a spell.
Maybe it's been this way since it was planted,
But one thing's clear: the blasted tree's enchanted."
"Then, since our pear tree evidently blights
The garden, let it be burnt to spare us further horrid sights,"
The wife observed. "Run in," she told the footman; "fetch some men
To chop it down. I'll not stand for its nonsense ever again."
The poor tree was attacked with ringing blows.

But what, the axemen wondered, had it done to earn
This sentence. "Just cut it down," the lady said. "The rest's not
   your concern."
Thus did Wife Two achieve her task (though Goodness knows
The tree perforce did more than serve its turn!)

On to the third one's trick. This lady had a passion for hilarity
Which led her to frequent a woman-friend's with regularity,
For in this household fun and games were the order of the day
And all the boys and girls came out to play.
Now she had a lover residing at present in the area,
And he took the view that pleasure must be untrammelled if it is
   to be complete,
So he proposed to the lady that a night alone together would be distinctly
   cheerier.
"Two nights," said she. "You'll not be incommoded for much less, my sweet!
Just leave it to me. As for my husband, I'll
See to losing of him for just a while."
No sooner said than done – and it's as well this lady was resourceful,
For her better half was an inveterate stay-at-home, and not the least
   remorseful
That he never travelled to Rome
In search of indulgences when he could come by them nearer home.
Now the young lady was quite the opposite; indeed maybe one of
   her strengths
Was the zeal and fervour with which, in the pursuit of her own indulgence,
   she'd go to inordinate lengths.
Pilgrimages galore she'd indulged in – but this was now so dated it was
   barely conceivable,
And what she needed next to make her mark was something altogether more
   recherché and less readily achievable.
That night she attached to her big toe a length of string
That led to the front door, then laid her down to sleep
Beside her husband Henry. Now as he turned over he felt it, and this was the
   vital thing,
For he was thus to leap

To the conclusion that some mischief was afoot. Pretending therefore
  to be fast asleep
He mused awhile, then up he got, tiptoed across the floor,
Leaving his wife in slumber that was not factitious
(Or so it seemed to him), and followed the string out through the door
Into the street, whence he concluded that he was right to be suspicious.
Some lover, he decided, would tug his lady by the toe
Thus conveying to her the message that he was present without and
  rearing to go.
Then the good woman would slip down, taking care that he, poor
  husband, was not woken –
What on earth could this contrivance else betoken?
Assuredly everything pointed to a cuckoo in the nest,
And if one thing was certain it was his total reluctance to make the
  man an honoured guest.
With this thought in mind he armed to the teeth and took up his station
  as sentry
Pacing up and down before the door, ready to apprehend such gentry
As came to tug the string. The reader, though, must appreciate
That in addition to the front door there was at the rear of the house
  a gate
Giving access, and a maid ready to extend
The welcome of the house to the expectant friend
– For in the matter of deceiving husbands, there's not a domestic
  averse
To taking the lady's part,
Knowing this to be the way to a plenary indulgence, to say nothing
  of her heart.
Therefore, while Henry paced the street and continued to disburse
His energy to catch the offender, the very same
Was in bed with the dame.
The night was passed in wholly pleasurable activity
And no alarms, thanks to the aforesaid maid's proclivity
To mind her mistress's business. Thus the young man, alerted
By this watchdog, fled the nest at the timely moment, and trouble
  was averted.
The husband returned at daybreak and climbed back into bed,

Explaining that he'd gone upstairs to sleep, as a migraine had been
    afflicting his head.
Two days later the wife again attached the string, Henry noticed and
    in high agitation
Left the room and resumed his station
While the lover resumed *his*, and the happy pair merrily frisked.
Then for a third time the trick was repeated, and Henry on the same excuse
Dashed out, leaving his place to the lover who of course put it to
    better use.
By now, though, passion was sated and our couple risked
No further such engagements; for all that they were proficient,
A drama in three acts was deemed sufficient.
Come midnight, though, the lover having deftly made
His escape, the string was tugged by one of his domestics, who was instantly
    waylaid
By the husband, grasped by the collar and, thus apprehended,
Marched indoors. Did the spouse but know it, the man who had offended
Was but a lowly footman, who played his role in this ingenious masquerade.
With the household subject to this unseemly perturbation
The wife ran down to Henry and required an explanation.
The footman threw himself down at their knees
Declaring that the chambermaid was the apple of his eye and his heart's ease.
As for the string, what that was for
Was so he could alert her to come and open the door,
And that quite recently they had both
Engaged to plight their troth.
"So that," said the wife to her maid with righteous indignation,
"Is why I caught you with a string upon your toe:
I did as you did, thus to trap your gallant with such an application.
Your husband, is he? Very well, out you go
This very night." Henry proved kinder, said this might wait till break of day.
The pair were accorded a large endowment, we discover,
The maid by the luckless Henry, the footman by the wily lover.
They then repaired to church, there to exchange their vows to love, to
    honour and obey.

The three tricks thus enacted, which one proved the best?
Well, don't ask *me* this question – I'll be blessed
If *I* know which. The lady charged with the wager's supervision
Was quite unable to come to a decision.
Each rightly thought she'd placed the winning bet:
The case, dear reader, 's not concluded yet.

(Derived in part from Boccaccio: *The Decameron*, VII.8 and VII.9)

The Old Crocks' Calendar

I've more than once been puzzled to observe
That when parents give a daughter's hand in marriage
The one provision that brings harmony to wedlock is the very one
    they will disparage.
Father and mother are uniquely interested to preserve
The patrimony – all else they regard with serene unconcern.
Tender young misses are paired off with elderly curmudgeons –
And yet watch their parents get a fit of the dudgeons
The moment they enter their carriage and discern
That the steeds in the shafts are of unequal size;
Or if they find that the dog a-courting
Their bitch has evaded a proper sorting,
They'll take good care that the two don't fraternise.
Your oxen in the yoke will always pull with equal strength,
For otherwise they'd be hard put to plough a single length
Of furrow. Well, couples in matrimonial yoke, if ill assorted,
Are bound to find their conjugal relations immeasurably thwarted,
Indeed they're bound to fail.
And thereby hangs a tale:

Richard of Quinzica was a man known for his evasion
Of his matrimonial duties by making a constant song
And dance about how such conjunctions were bad on ferial days, and
    on feast days utterly wrong –
And he remained quite deaf to all persuasion.
The fellow was a judge in Pisa, and a man well learnèd in the law;

Prosperous too but, greybeard that he was, he ought to have selected
A wife of approximately his own vintage. Instead he picked the most
    eligible, the best connected
And most youthful beauty in the entire city, and a girl whose tribe
    included a good score
Of Pisa's leading citizens. Now of course Richard ought never
To have married Linda, and for a judge this was not at all clever –
Indeed the town was soon rife with insinuators
All observing that the judge's children would not be short of paters.
Many's the man who sits in judgment and bestows
Counsel on others, but can't see further than his nose.
So the judge, who lacked the wherewithal to be of use
In bed to a young filly of Linda's temper, discovered the following excuse
To rein her in: there was not one day in the entire year
According to *his* calendar, when sexual congress might be enacted
    without fear
Or scruple – a fine pretext for elderly males, but grounds only for
    dissatisfaction
If you were a nubile female who liked to see a little action.
Did I say "not one day"? I meant "exceeding few"
And even that handful he would willingly eschew.
There was not a weekday without its religious connotation;
And saints were revered who'd yet to be invented.
"Friday of course is meant for penance, not for carnal celebration,"
Said he; and Saturday was not a day when he relented
"For is it not," said he, "the vigil of the Lord's day?
And God forgive the man who considers it a bawd's day.
Besides," he added, "I don't have to remind you that Sunday is the
    day of rest.
Monday? Oh, Heaven forbid we *start* the week with *that*!
The truly Christian soul will dedicate her every labour to the
    Lord's behest."
The other weekdays, too, furnished excuses which he had off pat.
But when it came to a solemn feast, that's when he truly shone –
Days in advance were devoted to abstention, and the embargo
    carried on
For several days after the feast had come and gone.

The Ember days were out, and so of course was the full extent
Of Advent and of Lent.
Such seasons were a time for God (and for old men, a gift of God withal).
He had an ample list of patron saints, and no quarter was given for
    a Doctor of the Church,
An Apostle or Evangelist. There was not a Virgin, Martyr or Confessor to
    leave him in the lurch –
He knew the feast days off by heart of all saints, great and small.
But if a day were proof against liturgical excuses he only had to say
"No, this won't do: today, my dear, is an unlucky day."
Or else it was too foggy, or the heat was unendurable:
One excuse or another was readily procurable.
This situation never varied, and it was barely four times a year
That by special dispensation the learnèd man endured to make a pair
With his belovèd – and even then he afforded her but the stingiest measure,
And scarcely calculated to give her pleasure.
Apart from this the judge did all within his power
To cosset his wife – clothes, jewels and trinkets were lavished on her
    in an absolute shower.
But all these ingenuous baubles failed to move her deeply:
Our Linda was not a girl to be won over quite so cheaply.

Now her husband owned a villa on the coast
And in the balmy season the one thing that pleased her most
Was to go and stay there – never less than once a week.
And what they both enjoyed was to take out a boat and seek
A little solace in fishing, not too far from shore.
So one day each of them took a boat – young Linda and her man of law –
With just one or two hands to crew; but firstly they laid bets
As to which of them would land the bigger catch in their own nets
And be attended by the better luck and enjoy a greater glory.
Who, though, should set his sights on Linda's dory
But a notorious pirate who was promptly to effect her capture.
The husband's craft was spared – but this occasioned him no rapture.
(The pirate's failure to embark the husband may occasion some surprise.
Maybe he dared venture no closer into the bay.
Or else perhaps he had the foresight to surmise

That Richard's presence would inhibit the enjoyment of his prey.
Here, you see, was a pirate who may have been avid for treasure,
But he was even more avid for pleasure,
And as he ploughed the seas in pursuit of his honourable vocation
He, like his fellows, kept a shipboard romance ever under consideration.
Seamen are always willing to do good; indeed they're normally
    reckoned to be a good sort,
And you'll not find any of *their* number letting saints' days interfere with
    their sport.)
Such then was our pirate, and he hailed from the Côte d'Azur,
Or so the chronicles aver.
Well, for a full half-day our captive beauty
Evinced distress in tears (as was consistent with her wifely duty)
While Pagano (the pirate) tendered consolation
Until the time was ripe for her capitulation.
Here was a man well practised in the arts
Of love, adept at boarding ships and breaking hearts.
Love took a hand, the greatest pirate known –
Abduction is his stock-in-trade, and quarter's seldom shown.
But Linda had her ransom counted out and ready to disburse,
And it was just as well she had the right money in her purse
For Pagano was not a man to recognise any vigil or feast
And as for her calendar with the days scored through in red, this was no
    longer of the least
Utility, she could forget it.
"No longer," said he, "let it
Dangle from your girdle." At table it might incur a mention
Now and then; for the rest, it claimed no more attention.

The husband Richard would have taken any bet
That his devoted wife remained chaste, intact and constant even yet,
And that, God willing, a payment would secure the girl's retrieval.
From Pagano he obtained a safe-conduct or *laissez passer*
And on arrival asked him, "How much shall I pay you for my lassie?
Just name your price." "Well, it's a shame that I'm accounted evil,"
The pirate said, "For look, the fact is I'm very handsome:
You're going to have your lady back without a ransom,

For God forbid that such a tender wedded amity
Should by my fault be blighted by calamity.
The lady you've moved heaven and earth to recover the moment she
    was lost
Will be restored to you as you desire and, moreover, at no cost.
Just let me see though, first, that she is yours:
The fact is, a good number of beauties come into my paws
And if I gave you back the wrong one, I'd feel somewhat to blame.
Now recently there was a tall young woman to whom I laid a claim;
She was fresh and well fleshed, with chestnut hair. If on sight of her
    she runs to your embrace,
Why, take her, there'll be nothing further to detain you in this place."
"This indeed," said Richard, "is very good to hear,
But your magnanimity is really more than I can bear.
We all of us have our living to make,
So set a price on the poor captive's head and I'll pay it – cash down
    and no mistake.
No need to beat about the bush. Look, here's my purse:
Just count the proceeds. I would not have you treat me better nor any worse
Than if I were a man of simply no account. Nay, I think I'd find you
    most unfeeling
If you could boast of having overreached me in fair dealing.
And as to this lady, be in no doubt that she is mine.
Don't take *my* word – she'll give the clearest sign:
Her frenzied kisses will attest the love that I inspire;
Alas, my only fear is lest for very joy at seeing me she may expire."
The wife was sent for; but her disposition
On seeing her husband was cool, unexcited and distinctly sober,
Nor did she evince the smallest sign of recognition –
He might as well have been a stranger from distant Manitoba.
"Look," said the judge, "the little creature's all bashful and coy
In front of others, and dares not show her feelings. Were I alone
You can be sure she would in haste atone
For this reserve, and fling her arms about me in a transport of joy."

"If that's all that it takes," said Pagano, "pray retire
Into the bedroom with her." Once within, the agèd squire

Shut the door and addressed his wife in the words I here report:
"Come Linda, I am none other than Richard, your constant husband and
    true model of devotion.
Come, look at me. Do you find me so greatly altered? Ah, but you've
    no notion
What sorrow occasioned by your abduction has done to distort
My features. Now tell me: have I ever refused you any treat, any payment,
Be it for your entertainment, or your raiment?
Have I ever failed to be a good sport? A slave to your smallest whim?
Slave! Why, you're the one who'll be a slave if you remain with *him*!
Besides, do you have absolutely no care for your reputation?"
"Is this the time to take *that* into consideration?"
Enquired Linda tartly. "Did it enter anybody's reckoning
When you stood out there a-beckoning
And quite against my wishes I was married off to an old dotard like you,
Never mind that I was a vigorous young woman who might have
    considered herself due
For a less unattractive old party,
And one whose performance in bed was considerably more hale
    and hearty.
For such entertainment I was, I think, sufficiently well inclined
And have to say, *entre nous*, that I was quite adequately designed
To accept my partner's ministrations.
But little had I reckoned with such a husband's calculations.
I took a husband whose only concern was whether it was a festival
    or feria,
While Pagano had barely ravished me before he showed me that
    all days could be a great deal merrier,
And in two days he taught me more of life
Than ever I learnt from four years as your wife.
So let me be, dear husband, and above all don't insist
On my return. I tell you, in this house calendars are never missed.
You and my kinsfolk have deserved a good deal worse:
You because you married me without first reckoning up your
    vital juices;
They for putting the brittle ties of wealth ahead of wedlock's
    other uses.

Why, next to yours and theirs, Pagano's is a bottomless purse.
And if statutes, canons, pandects form part of his lexicon –
Then I'm a Mexican.
But if I'm not mistook,
You could do worse than take a leaf out of his book.
He'll tell you this very morning how matters stand, and maybe pass
    you a few tips.
You look surprised and pained by this avowal. Well, there's no use
    pouting your lips
Or inferring that Linda tells a lie.
Now, since we are unwitnessed, here's the time to bid you and your
    festive days goodbye.
I'm made of flesh and blood; clothes don't alter that, however much
    they flatter me –
Between the head and heel, sir, are other parts to the anatomy!"
She had no more to say and, after so rude an awakening, the hapless
    lawyer
Was only glad to be able to make his escape from the pirate's foyer,
While our Linda, having thus delivered herself of a piece of her mind,
Needed no second invitation from Pagano to remain behind.
Poor Richard was left so shattered that, what with this
Added to the afflictions that wait upon old age,
He not many days later gave up the ghost and quit the stage,
Leaving the widow free to accept from her pirate a connubial kiss.

All to the good: neither suffered the mischance that Richard had
    incurred,
For each had first enjoyed the other on approval – a lesson to leave all
    greybeards sufficiently deterred,
Unless they are prepared to extend unbounded toleration,
In which case the favoured lover will ensure the lady's full
    gratification.

(Derived from Boccaccio: *The Decameron*, II.10)

A Lover Outwits a Mercenary Mistress

A man may get himself plucked clean by a seductive wench,
But that's no cause to rub our eyes and blench:
Nothing is for nothing, and Love always presents the bill to pay,
For amorous dalliance is reckoned up in silver coinage and in no
    other way.
Well, that's the fair sex for you. In this tale, however, I propose to
    address
This question, and for our honour's sake redress
The balance, for there is the odd occasion when a man's cunning
    is pitted
Against a wily woman's and *she* remains outwitted.

For my example I'll turn to one Gulfardo, a true reluctant spender.
He had his way with a flirtatious creature
And so successfully contrived to overreach her
That for all her favours she obtained not one cent of legal tender.
Thus take good note, you lusty blades, and keep it well in mind –
Not that such a ploy is needed by gentlemen of your persuasion,
Seeing that at court I could turn up Gulfardos by the dozen on the
    first occasion.
Now our hero frequented his friend Caspar, and the result was, he
    became amorously inclined
Towards Caspar's wife, a rare young beauty
Who charmed all comers and had but one fault: she felt it was her duty
To be forever increasing her tidy pile;
And that this trait put off her suitors is a fact beyond denial.

This in our day is no uncommon failing.
I've said it before: Languorous sighs may be all very well
But he who comes to press his suit will find his efforts unavailing
If he arrives not cash in hand – his words will prove quite foreign to
    the belle.
Cupid's store is crammed with all that's wanted for gambling, flirting,
    every dissipation,
Indeed with all it needs to make more cuckolds in our nation
Than heroes spilling from the Trojan horse in days of yore.
But to return to our exacting lady: The prospective lover
Could make no headway until he uttered certain words. What these
    were you'll presently discover.
I'll say only that certain well minted arguments have the force of law.
Gulfardo spoke them, and his words added up to two hundred crowns.
So neatly turned a speech sufficed to dissipate her frowns.
Whence did the lad obtain them? Why, from his good friend
Young Caspar who, on the point of leaving for the country, was willing
    to lend
The sum without for a moment suspecting that it was to pass
So quickly to his wedded lass.
The cash was handed over in the presence of a witness.
"Here," said Gulfardo, "are the two hundred crowns that are to be
    returned
To your spouse." The lady detected in these words a certain fitness,
Assuming they were spoken to disguise the nature of the pact wherein
    she was concerned.
Be it said, she kept her word and, the next day, proved herself
    unsparing
In the bestowal of her favours; indeed what he found endearing
Was her willingness to give full measure and a little also in advance,
For the handsome payer deserves to be accorded all he wants.

With Caspar returned from his estates, Gulfardo waited
Upon his friend, the wife being present at the meeting,
And said to him, after a cordial greeting:
"I have repaid your wife the loan: the urgent business it anticipated

Has, contrary to expectations, fallen through.
So please discharge the debt and give me back my I.O.U."
The lady thus had to acknowledge the repayment of the bill –
She had no choice, the man had witnesses. And yet, if looks could
    kill . . . !
Besides, the thing that most upset the missus
Was to have been duped into bestowing all those supplementary kisses.
It must be said she bitterly repented
Her bounty in view of the lost income these all represented.
The lover took his leave and off he went to spread the news,
To trumpet and proclaim it, to publish and blazon it abroad.
Go on and blame him, reader, if you choose –
Among us Frenchmen discretion is a virtue generally ignored.

(Derived from Boccaccio: *The Decameron*, VIII.1)

Hans Carvel's Ring

When Hans Carvel took a wife, he was already in his dotage, to
    be truthful,
Whereas the girl was, seen from whichever angle, youthful.
This of course gave him more than enough to put him in a stew:
Such alliances generally do.
Babeau, to give the young female her name,
(She was the daughter of the local beak)
Was spunky, voluptuous and by no definition tame,
And for bedtime grapplings she had absolutely the correct physique.
Now Carvel, with a natural aversion to cuckoldry and to being made
    to look a fool,
Served up to the young creature a concoction or gruel
Taken from all the best texts, not forgetting legends and Holy Writ.
Secret trysts were, of course, one of those things that made him spit.
With all the impedimenta of temptation he proved censorious,
All those beauty tips and hints, so much instruction
Towards seduction
Left him feeling the reverse of euphorious.
If the little flirt was brought to heel by any such lecture
I'll leave you to conjecture –
The only talk she found that didn't tire her
Was sweet-talk from an admirer.
Of course her not caring a feather
Had the poor man quite at the end of his tether;
I mean when you're that far down on your luck it
's enough to make a fellow want to kick the bucket.

However, in his aggrievement
He did come to his moment of relievement.
What follows may sound squalid,
But its veracity is rock-solid.
One night, after sitting down to a meal characterised by
      rude plenty,
And knocking back maybe one firkin more of the new vintage than
      he'd meant, he
Was in bed beside Babeau and snoring before you could count to
      twenty,
When he dreamed that there was Satan
A-waitin'.
Satan, putting a ring on his finger, addressed him thus:
"Well it seems, old chap, you've worked yourself into a bit of a fuss,
And I'm a soft touch, as you know.
Here, take this ring and never let it go:
For so long as you keep it tight
On your finger everything will come out right . . .
I mean, there'll be no risk of her bestowing it
Without your knowing it."
"Sir," said Carvel, "you have my gratitude
For such an understanding attitude;
So great's the favour that you have accorded,
I trust Your Bounteousness will be suitably rewarded."
With this, out from his sleep he started drifting
And as from his bleary eyes the veil was lifting,
O happy dreamer! say you. Not a jot:
He found his finger stuck in Babeau's ———.

(Derived from *Cent Nouvelles Nouvelles*, Tale 11)

Fair Exchange . . .

There's nothing like a change of fare to assure a man of satisfaction;
And when I say "man", the term must here be taken to embrace the
   daughters of Eve.
Moreover I've no idea why Rome has failed so far to accord us leave
To indulge – if we are married – in a little barter or similar transaction.
Maybe not as often as one might wish, but at any rate once in one's life
It would be good to be able to exchange one's wife.
Perhaps one day such a licence will be granted, and I say Amen to this:
Believe me, here in France such a papal indult would not come amiss,
Seeing that your Frenchman goes in for barter every day.
It's simply that the Lord created him that way.

Once upon a time near Rouen (a city wherein Wisdom has long been
   wont to settle),
There was a village, and here two rustics lived with wives of rudest
   health and in the finest fettle.
Now such folk are scarcely models of refinement, and it is beyond
   dispute that Love's
Never been inclined to pamper them or handle their sort with kid gloves.
It so happened, nonetheless, that the pair of them were finding their
   spouses tedious and their marriages lacking in zest,
And one rest-day, as they sat with their neighbour the notary before their
   respective tankards of the best
Local brew, one of the two observed: "Master Desmond, sir, you find me
   indulging in a speculation that is mildly diverting.
You will in your day have drawn up all manner of contracts and deeds;

How about drawing one whereby a person exchanges his wife, the way
    some people exchange their steeds?
Our rector has, after all, just changed his parish. Is that so very
    different from concerting
To change one's spouse? By no means! Father Gregory's constant refrain,
    I believe I am right in asserting
Was that he was wedded to his flock. And yet he has chosen another!
Let us therefore do likewise – what say you then, good brother?"
"Most willingly," replied the second yokel. "But it is clear to anybody
    who has eyes
That when it comes to beauty it is my missus who carries off the prize,
So I put it to you, Master Desmond, sir, you would be entitled to consider
    me a fool
If I didn't require a makeweight from my neighbour in the shape of
    his mule."
"My mule! Now wait a minute!" cried the first. "There's not a
    woman on the face of this earth
That does not know her worth.
A woman is not a creature to be gone over inch by inch with a
    fine-tooth comb –
And yours is not a whit superior to the one *I* have at home.
My mule, you say? Why, he's the king of mules – and, Stephen,
    you'd not get me to concede
Even my donkey! No makeweight, this must be a straight exchange.
    Agreed?"
Now up spoke Desmond, the notary, after due consideration:
"What if Stephanie has the advantage over Jeannette, at least so
    people say?
To my mind the best of a creature is not what is put on display.
For my taste there is a good deal more to a woman that is not
    susceptible to observation.
Besides, a lass may prove deceptive, and it's as well not to submit her at
    once to a too-close inspection.
Come therefore, neighbours, let us have everything clear and out in
    the open,
For neither of you wishes to buy a pig in a poke, and indeed here's what
    I'm hopin':

Let's set your two young consorts side by side and view them just as the
    Good Lord made 'em – if you've no objection."

The expedient was not to everybody's taste: it was not what certain people
    wished to hear,

And you would soon have seen two husbands vying with each other to
    rehearse their partners' graces.

"You'll find no fault in my filly," said Stephen, "I don't care how you put
    her through her paces,

There's not a blemish to her from fetlock to the tip of the ear."

"Well my Jeannette," said Giles; "her little body's clean as a whistle,
    if you choose to inspect her.

I'm telling you, she's a real cup of nectar."

"Now my Stephanie," maintained her spouse, "she's as supple as an osier,

And if your woman's nectar, well mine is sheer ambrosia!"

"Well, listen to me, my friend," the other said. "When it comes to
    playtime . . . if you know what I mean,

You don't know my Jeannette – she'll show you tricks that you'll
    have never seen!"

This made young Stephen scoff. "Huh? Wait till I tell you about
    me and Stef,

Then maybe you'll pipe down and save your bref.

There's but one thing that makes us argumentative

And that is, which of us 's the more inventative.

Give it a couple of days – you'll see for yourself by and by.

Meanwhile, old mate, here's mud in your eye!"

Tankards were raised (or were they glasses?)

To drink the health of the two wedded lasses,

And the deal was struck, the bargain was concluded –

But not before the mule had been included

As a makeweight. "No trouble at all," the notary assured

The two young men, "and it's as well to say

This kind of contract's drawn up every day!"

He was a genial soul, was Desmond, and while his piece of parchment
    undoubtedly incurred

A generous fee, who paid it? Not the husbands – for Desmond thought it
    smarter

To charge it to the wives who were the object of this barter.

The rustics thought it wise to hush things up, but Fate
Determined that the priest get wind of it, and no cleric was ever faster
To assert his rule than the present village pastor.
I shan't be categorical, indeed I was not there, but when it comes to throw-
    ing their weight
About and wielding a rod of iron,
Our clergy partake a good deal less of the lamb than they do of the lion,
And to leave his authority thus flouted occasioned in this pastor a
    profound distaste –
But was there ever a priest who allowed his edicts to go to waste?
In the village, however, our two yokels could not conclude their
    negotiation
Without occasioning the most eloquent disapprobation
So they thought it best to pull up sticks and transfer fairly quickly to
    a new location
Where all at first went well, God willing, and in fact to be a peasant
With a bartered bride was, on the face of it, quite pleasant.
The wives, be it observed, proved no less zestful than their husbands
    in this matter,
And as they went about their daily rounds they would often stop to chatter.
"Tell me, my dear," they'd say to each other, "don't you find this
    new observance
Suits us deliciously?
What if we go another step and now exchange our servants?"
If this last did take place, it took place surreptitiously.
As for the first, it suited them so well that when the initial month
    was over
They were all of them still in clover.
Eventually, though, the business started to become less appetising,
And if Stephen was the first to weary of it, this will scarcely be surprising:
He hankered for his Stephanie, and felt he was the one who'd come
    off worst.
As for Giles, what he missed was the mule thrown in to make the weight,
And yet he'd never have agreed that the exchange now be reversed.
What then? Out in the woods one day young Steve espied his late
Lamented Stef all on her own within a hazel copse, secluded and apart;
There she was, napping by the banks of a murmuring stream.

The lad drew near; this woke her with a start
And, quite forgetful of her bartered situation, it would seem,
She let the gallant come down to brass tacks without the least resistance –
In a word, the pair of them were quick to go the distance
And he discovered in her a wholly new vitality,
Greater indeed than in the first days of their conjugality.
Why so? What a question! In love, bread filched and eaten on the sly
Tastes better than bread bought from any baker's shop –
Ask those who are more learnèd in this theme than I.
Besides, it cannot but be thus, if you really stop
To think of it. Wedlock and the Love-god are not folk to be a-baking
Their loaves in the same oven, witness the antics that we have seen taking
Place within the hazel copse.
They truly made a feast of it, they pulled out all the stops
For, bear in mind, when it comes to culinary expertise
Old Wedlock doesn't reach to Cupid's knees:
The Love-god's palate is refined, and not a dish was there for savouring
But Cupid had attended to its flavouring.
Once Stephanie departed, Stephen, to whom all this was new,
Said to himself: "I do believe
Young Giles must have a trick or two
Kept up his sleeve.
I find that my recent wife
Is prettier than I've ever seen her in her life.
Clearly this deal no longer passes muster;
Let's welsh on it, let's resort to bullying and to bluster."
Here, then, was the plan that his scheming mind evoked:
He'd go to his partner and have the exchange revoked.
Giles, however, was not the man to take it lying down,
And at all events this was the point when an emissary was sent
        from town,
An envoy from the Bishop's court, who took the case in hand
With the result, predictably, that the business was noised throughout
        the land.
Parliament decided that the question fell exclusively within its own
        commission:

Desmond, who drew the deeds, was summoned to the bar to make
    a deposition,
And that, so people say, is now where matters stand –
The incident, you see, has only recently occurred.
Poor neighbour Stephen! A pity he has no more brains than has a bird!
If the poor fellow had not been so dense
He'd not have pulled the rug from under his own feet:
By stating that his games with Stephanie left him replete
With pleasure, it followed that the woman simply could not be his wife;
    so it only made sense
To leave the girl to Giles. And this still left the hazel bower,
Whither Stephanie, they say, would frequently repair,
A song in her heart and not a care
In the world: To make a tryst with her was well within young Stephen's
    power.
Very well, let's suppose it was not quite
So easy: good, that would merely serve to whet his appetite.
But just try preaching this message to the unlettered!
The fact remains that what they did was good (indeed, could not be
    bettered)
Without retrieving what they had exchanged. Many's the man who could
    do worse than take a leaf
Out of their book. Were I not past it, *I*'d be more than lief!

The Head-dress

Nuns, suffer me one last time to give you a place in this my compilation
Despite myself. Accounts of your good deeds abound, and merit
    universal approbation,
Enjoying as they do a charisma not to be found in any other similar
    relation.
Just one more, then, and that (I think you'll not dispute)
Makes three. But stay! I'm out by one. The total's four.
Come, let us count them up: Masetto, the gardener who played the mute;
The abbess in need of a handsome lad to cure her as she languished
    at death's door;
The present tale, which is not to be regarded
As the most innocent. And that of Sister Jeanne, the nun who was
    unable to resist
Making a baby – that certainly is not to be discarded.
So there they are: four is the number to make up the list.
"Is it not bizarre that you assign to us so large a place
In this book of yours? Why, it's an absolute disgrace!"
I hear you all object.
Believe me, it's nothing of *my* doing. What do you expect?
Whoever made this choice it was not *me*. What's more you will forgive
    me when I mention
That if you paid your breviaries the proper share of your attention
You'd simply have no business nor acquaintance with these tales –
In truth the former weigh too lightly in your scales!
Onwards, then, without a further moment's hesitation
To the following narration.

There was once a person who was the regular frequenter
Of a convent of nuns. He was a youth with a healthy appetite, it seems,
    for birds of such a feather.
One sister in particular admired him, indeed he sent 'er
Into raptures; she would devour him with her eyes, beam at him, and
    when they were together,
Behaved all coyly and would say, "Your humble servant, sir," and danced
Attendance on him – not that this left their situation much advanced.
There was (so the story goes) not a nun, whether still in bud or already
    with grey hairs,
In whose mind this boy did not occasion certain intimate ideas.
The sighing was pervasive, a matter that did not escape his observation
Though he did not let this cause him serious vexation.
Sister Isabel had the young man for her entire fruition,
As well she might, being a person of most charming disposition;
Moreover here was a bird but newly fledged; and if one were to enlarge
Upon her virtues one would mention her beauty, and her nicely
    filled corsage.
Thus if she inspired envy among her sisters and had them up in arms,
This was on two counts: her lover, and her charms.
As she pursued her amours, the rest of the community was drawn
To spy on her: no profit without loss, no rose without a thorn.
The sisters spied on her so closely in their efforts at detection
That one dark night, propitious to expressions of affection –
For with such secret business, darkness is generally preferred –
Certain words were overheard
In the monastic cell
Of Sister Isabel,
A certain voice could be made out that gave expression
To certain sentiments not to be found inside the breviary she had in
    her possession.
"Hark! It's the lover!" they all cried. "Quick, we've got him trapped!"
And (with a sentry posted) off the whole swarm ran, all up in arms and
    buzzing with excitement,
To bring to Mother Abbess the indictment.
They reached her door. Triumphantly they rapped
Upon it: "Madam, arise! Our Sister Isabel,"

They said, "Has got a male in her cell!"
Now at this juncture it needs to be said
That Mother Abbess was not at her prayers, nor sleeping. She was
     entertaining in her bed
The local priest, old Father John. So, before she stepped forth and faced
The sisters, to avoid giving them grounds for mistrust, she rose in haste,
And groped about her for her veil. Well, in the absence of light,
(For all this happened, of course, at night,)
What she picked up was the reverend's breeches, the sort of mistake
A person incurs who is not sufficiently awake.
This error was, alas, to prove in its consequences less than paltry
When she donned this garment thinking it was her psaltery.*
So here was the abbess wearing trousers for a veil
And, thus bedecked, desired to hear a second repetition of the tale.
This done, she spoke in irritation: "Why, the insolence of it! By Heaven,
     it can't be borne:
We cannot let our convent be infected by such a devil's spawn,
God forbid! Indeed, we'll call the girl to order," she stated with a frown.
"Summon the chapter, then just watch me give the minx a thorough
     dressing down!"

A chapter thus was held, since this abbess liked to summon chapters,
And Isabel was duly brought in by her captors
To where the Reverend Mother sat amidst her council, or her diet,
Whereupon, in the ensuing quiet,
All that could be heard were the tears of the hapless little goose,
Which coursed down cheeks that (she recalled) her scapegrace lover had
     just put to other use.
"What!" cried the abbess. "A man? In here, among
The sisters? Oh what a scandal for our holy congregation!
Come, why are you not already dead of sheer humiliation?
Tell me, who made you give a welcome to that piece of dung?
Now Isabel (and bear in mind that Sister is no longer a name
To which you are entitled to lay claim),

* A psaltery, being in shape an inverted trapeze, provided the familiar appellation
  For the distinctive head-dress worn by the religious of this congregation. (Trans.)

Isabel, you may not be aware of the chastisement visited by this court
On miscreants of your sort.
You'll know before tomorrow dawns. Now speak!"
Well, the poor little nun could only hang her head in shame. All this talk
    made her weak
At the knees; quite mortified and penitent, she could scarcely have been
    charier
To raise her eyes and look on her Superior.
But by happy chance, what caught her eye when she did look up, was the
    trousered head
Which had entirely escaped the observation
Of the rest of the community as they all listened, rapt, to the lady's
    peroration,
And focused their attention carefully on everything she said.
A happy chance for Isabel, I say. She saw the sight and, steadying
    her nerve,
Was prompted very sweetly to observe:
"Ah, Mother dear, your psaltery: how very strangely it appears to dangle.
Pray do adjust it to a more becoming angle."
Maybe the lady's aglet, which often served for stud, had hooked
The garment; at all events the veil was not unlike a pair
Of breeches, though young Isabel, for whom both veil and trousers were
    freshly printed in the mind, was quite aware,
Beyond mistaking them, of how each garment looked.
(Be it said in passing, the raiment wherewith the reverend's nether
    quarters were attired
Was of a different cut from that worn by a young Lothario who wished to
    be admired.)
"The creature dares to joke," the abbess said. "Oh, the insolence of it, the
    audacity!
Disgraced with sinfulness, she's not a whit submissive; and when
    we chastise her
Does she repent? Why no – she only demonstrates a fresh pugnacity!
What does the monster think: that we should canonise her?
You leave my veil alone, you daughter of damnation,
You little ember of the eternal fires, and give your mind to the instant
    reparation

Of your immortal soul." She rounded off her sermon with many a force-
   ful objurgation
That would have made another creature quail,
But all that Sister Isabel would say was: "Madam, do adjust your veil."
Well, prompted by this reckless daring,
The whole flock raised their eyes and started staring;
The younger sisters grinned and smirked,
Their elders sputtered, and the erstwhile lecturer, supremely irked,
Now suddenly fell silent in vexed mortification, which is hardly strange
When she considered the untoward exchange
Of headgear. The lady was quite at a loss for words. Meanwhile, with the
   sisters all a-twitter,
The Reverend Mother reckoned it was fitter
To adjourn the chapter. Therefore this is what she said:
"It's too late now to take a vote. The thing must wait till morning.
   Now off you go to bed!"

The next day, for sufficient reason, passed without the holding of
   a chapter,
And the second day as well, for the convent's wiser heads took the view
That silence was indubitably apter,
And that nothing but disaster would ensue
From too much agitation. If wretched Isabel remained the object
   of hostility,
That was only because she was envied the possession of her lover
   in tranquillity.
The other nuns, after failing to persuade her to give them all a share,
Dreamed of a gallant of their own, and made to look elsewhere –
Indeed, the rediscovery of former beaux became a convent-wide
   obsession.
Thus, with the youth abandoned to Isabel with full right of possession,
And the other
(I mean the pastor) devised without demur unto the Reverend Mother,
The communal accord now readily contrived
To find a lover for each sister who would otherwise have been deprived.

(Derived from Boccaccio: *The Decameron*, IX.2)

The Impossible Task

A devil, whose wickedness exceeded even his guile,
Prepared a charm for a young wooer that proved quite satisfactory:
It enabled him to conquer a lady who for a considerable while
Had been proving most hard-hearted and refractory.
The lover's pact with the demon required that his belovèd must relent
And he was to enjoy her favours to his heart's content.
"I'll soon have your lady tractable, but there is one condition"
– So said this spirit of perdition –
"Instead of your obeying Satan's commands once he has done you this
  favour with a spell,
He will come to *you* for orders and do at once whatever it is you tell
Him to do. Then, after such an introduction,
Your demon-slave will be right back to fulfil your next instruction.
This you must give without a moment's hesitation,
And as this compact starts, so will it be in its continuation.
Delay one second, and it will no longer be your lady who owns you
  body and soul: it will be Old Nick.
He'll be along to fetch you double quick,
And thus you'll be disposed of in accordance with his inclination."
The lover readily assented, for it goes without saying,
Giving orders is twenty times more easy than obeying.

The lover, having arrived at this conclusion,
Went off to find his lady and won from her favours in the amplest
  profusion;

He tasted pleasures quite beyond compare,
And all was utter bliss, were it not for that devil forever at his ear.
The lad would bid him do the first thing that came into his mind:
Build him a palace, raise a storm – in a twinkling the devil had done the
    task he'd been assigned.
Coins rained into his purse quite without stinting,
For the devil was a practised hand at minting.
He'd send the creature off to Rome; the brute would hasten back
With a thick pile of pardons in his sack.
He never took long over a journey. Nothing was too hard.
Now all this having to cudgel his wits in search of new orders left the
    poor lover's brain quite scarred.
He plaintively brought his problem to his voluptuous friend,
And told her the entire tale from beginning to end.
"Why, what a fuss for so little!" said she. "I have what it takes
To cure this canker in a brace of shakes.
When Satan comes, just give him what I'm holding in my hand,
And make him understand
You want the thing uncrinkled – never mind if he has to work at it early
    and late,
You do not want it back until he's made it straight."
This said, she handed him what she had culled in that fairies' labyrinth,
    the grove
Of Venus, the same desirable object that in ancient Greece
The valiant Argonauts manfully strove
To seize: I mean the golden fleece.
(A sacred talisman worshipped by a noble prince: lest anybody spurn it, he
Made it the symbol of a knightly confraternity.)
"This object," said the lover to the devil, "is full of twists and loops, as
    you can well descry;
We want you to take out the curves and leave it straight as a die.
Now off with you and get to work." The devil left at once, the sooner
    to address
The task of placing the hair beneath a press.
He took a heavy hammer and gave it many a clout
In the hope of flattening it out,

And then decided to invoke
A tub of water to take the bends out by means of a good soak,
But all to no avail. Whatever stratagem, whatever secret or spell
    he applied,
'Twas all time wasted, he found his every effort was defied
By that bit of fleece. It would resist
All the elements, the rain, the wind, the snow or mist.
The more the devil worked at it, the less the object of his toil
Showed itself ready to uncoil.
"My stars, what can this be!" the demon would say.
"I have never even once
In my born days come across a contrivance made this way –
It makes the most fiendishly clever fiend look like a dunce!"
One fine morning Satan paid the young man a visit
And said: "All right, I quit. Only tell me first, just what the devil is it?
Here, have it back. And let's be honest, I'm beaten – the blasted thing's
    still curly."
"Well, sir, I really think you're giving up a little prematurely.
This one is not alone: it has countless siblings who'd have been
    overjoyed
To see you kept so constantly employed."

Eel Pâté

Be it never so exquisite, beauty, if changeless, leads to surfeit.
Too much of a good thing is definitely less than perfeit.
Just give me a regular change of fare: this plainly will suffice –
Variety, you see, is my device.
Take my mistress, who's rather sallow of complexion:
Well, she's pure sunshine in my eyes, she suits me to perfection.
Why so? She's only recently acquired,
Whereas the one of whom I'm hitherto possessed,
For all that she is blessed
With a milk-white pallor, is no longer ardently admired,
Indeed she scarcely causes me the smallest palpitation,
And when she's saying Yes, my heart's responding No.
"Whence so?"
You ask, and you deserve an explanation,
Though I have said it once, so now you'll hear it twice:
Variety, you see, is my device.
(According to the spirit of this my assertion
It needs to be propounded in more than a single version,
So you, dear reader, will not deem it a disgrace
When I explain to you: *Variety* is my devace.)

It was that, too, of a man whose wife was a ravishing beauty;
He found himself wholly cured of love when it began to resemble
    a duty,
And after he had drawn from her a generous ration
Of delight, wedlock and undisputed possession extinguished his passion.

Now the man had a footman whose wife was a bonny little creature,

And the master, being a sociable sort, laid hold of the girl without even
needing to beseech 'er.

The footman thought ill of this and, as a matter of fact,

Asserted, on catching the pair in the act,

That as he was the one to have wed her

He was the only party now entitled to bed her.

My, did the foolish fellow make a song and dance, and call his wife
every name under the sun –

This sort of dalliance is not unusual, when all is said and done.

God save us from a worse disaster

Than having a lady's man for master!

The man harangued his master thus: "It's not, good sir, as though
I am possessive,

But mark my word: To each his own, sir – this is not excessive,

Indeed 'tis a refrain approved in equal part by God and Reason.

You have no woman? Does that entitle you to come a-seizin'

Mine, when you possess here in this house

A wife who must be worth a hundred of my unassuming spouse.

So spare yourself, good sir. It is too great an honour

For my wife to see the likes of you setting his cap upon 'er,

Nay this must quite exceed

That which I take to be her need.

Let us each confine ourselves to the person with whom we have elected
to dwell,

And pray forbear, sir, to dip your bucket in another's well;

Your own is brimful, and you bask in plenty –

A fact attested by the cognoscenti.

If the Good Lord had been so lavish as to accord to me the lady to
whom your troth is plighted

Well, I should have been delighted;

I should cleave to her and, though you, sir, may think this strange,

I would not accept even a duchess in exchange.

But what's done cannot be undone, so I would merely suggest (with
no offence intended)

You stick to the dish you have before you and stay away from mine as
a course to be entirely commended."

To this tirade the servant's master neither assented nor dissented;
He simply remained contented
To decree that a dish of eel pâté was to be placed before the footman at
    each day's meal,
This being a delicacy which held a quite particular appeal
To the man's palate. The first and second time he ate it up with relish,
But when it came to the third, the mere smell of it filled him with disgust.
"Whatever happens," said he, "I simply must
Eat other fare!" But, this not being permitted, he found his life becoming
    absolutely hellish.
"This," he was told, "is what our master is ordaining.
It has to be the fare to which you are confined;
You love it, don't you? So you'd better stop complaining."
"Damn it I've had enough," the servant whined.
"My palate's cloyed and caked
With pâté: why can't the wretched eel be baked
Just for a change? To dine off pâté days on end, why, it breeds aversion,"
    – that is what he said –
"And now I'd sooner be contented with a crust of bread:
Come, you can surely spare a piece of yours.
As for these horrid pâtés, take them away and toss them out of doors;
The stuff, so help me God, will use its best endeavour
To follow me to heaven . . . or wherever!"

This sudden outburst by the footman brought
His master running, and he, disposed to join in the sport,
Observed: "My friend, your attitude is not at all expectable
For one who finds this dish so perfectly delectable!
It now disgusts you? Have I not heard from your own lips a sonorous
    endorsal
When you've described this food as being your favourite morsel?
This sudden change of taste,
Good sir, has come about with quite unseemly haste!
Have I behaved in any stranger fashion? You hold me all to blame
For altering my diet, and consider me capricious
For tiring of what you hold to be delicious.

Well, are you not now doing just the same?
I'm teaching you, my friend, that, when it comes to appetite,
A man may well prefer to set aside the white
Loaf and reach across the table for a slice
Of brown. *Variety*, you see, is my device!"

Once his master had concluded his peroration
The footman experienced more than an ounce of consolation,
Not that he felt the argument left his case in pieces,
For, after all, is it enough for a man to allege no more than the pursuit
    of his caprices?
You welcome change? No harm in this, whichever way it's viewed,
But first of all you are to make it your mission,
If you can, to win over the party with whom you might come into
    opposition:
That is undoubtedly the path to be pursued.
As a matter of fact I believe that it is not in question
But that the partisan of change fell in with this suggestion.
He spoke with the tongue of angels, we are told,
And every word he used had first been dipped in gold.
In love, success will be assured
Where gilded words are used: this maxim's constant, and applies
    across the board.
Now all of you will understand the drift of my remark.
The point is one I've laboured in and out of season,
But not without good reason:
On this I cannot hold my peace, nor let my reader flounder in the dark,
And to the very end I'll see this maxim more than clearly stated:
In love your words will carry – if they are gold-plated.
Such words will always be sufficient to persuade
The lady and her lap-dog and her maid –
And not infrequently, let it be said,
The gentleman to whom the lady's wed.
Well, on this particular occasion
That gentleman was the only person to require persuasion,
And he proved more than willing to take note
Of eloquence to match the best of what the classic rhetors wrote!

The jealous spouse, who once had been so touchy and defiant
Became quite pliant.
It is even alleged that he adopted his master's commutations
And constantly replaced the object of his casual flirtations,
Indeed the stout fellow's attention to the ladies was now unflagging
And gave abundant cause to keep the gossips' tongues a-wagging.
The lad became a resolute collector
Of hearts, like the bee who goes from bloom to bloom in search of nectar,
And unfailingly it was his latest acquisition
In whom he found the highest level of fruition.
Matron and maid, the shy and the coquette,
They one and all alighted in his net.
Fastidious he was not: any was worth the effort to entice –
Variety, you see, was his device.

(Derived from *Cent Nouvelles Nouvelles*, Tale 10)

The Matron of Ephesus

If there is one tale that has grown quite threadbare from reiteration
It is the very one I here propose to tell in words of my own choosing.
"Why this one, sir? There's really no excusing
Such a choice. No one is forcing you to settle on this particular
    narration.
Has it not already spawned more versions than anyone can count?
What makes you think that yours is likely to amount
To anything? Why, sir, your venture smacks of the felonious:
Do you really fancy that *your* Matron will be an improvement upon
    that of old Petronius?
How can you dare to take the view
That yours will offer readers anything that's new?"
Well, I'll not bandy words with my critics, for this leads to nothing but
    oaths and curses;
Rather let us see if I can't give the old tale a new lease of life in these
    my verses.

Once upon a time there lived in Ephesus a lady whose equal was
    nowhere to be found
For goodness and virtue, and she had brought to the marital bond an
    added lustre,
(And when this is the case, the word tends to get around).
Nobody talked of anything except this lady and her chastity, and there
    was a constant muster

Of folk on their way to pay calls on her and to exhibit her as a rare object
    of their highest estimation:
She was the honour of her sex and the pride and joy of the Ephesian
    nation.
Mothers-in-law pointed her out to daughters-in-law as the one true object
    for their emulation,
While every Ephesian bridegroom vied
In commending her each to his respective bride.
And it was to her that the ancient and celebrated Academy of Prudes
    looked for its origin and inspiration.
Her husband loved her with a passion that was beyond all telling.
But he died. (The manner of his death is not a detail upon which it is
    worth dwelling.)
He died, and his will was lavish with bequests that were calculated
    to afford
Consolation to a widow, were it possible for anything to fill
The place of a spouse as adoring as he was adored.
This said, many's the widow who makes herself look as if she's been
    through the mill
While not neglecting to take a careful reckoning of what was in her dear
    departed's will –
However much she feels bereft,
Her tears are measured with a calculation of all that she's been left.
Now this one shrieked as if the world had come apart,
She made enough commotion to penetrate the hardest heart,
For all that it is generally considered, at these sorrowful junctures, that
    however immense
The despair that burdens the soul, it is always less intense
Than the weeping that attests it. These shows of desperation
Are seldom unaccompanied by a degree of ostentation.
All persons approaching this afflicted lady as she pursued her
    mourning
Felt it their duty to issue a timely warning
That everything had its limits, and her lamentation
Really ought not to be carried to exaggeration –
All of which merely served to achieve the widow's ultimate prostration.

Eventually, refusing to rejoice in the light of which her husband was
    deprived
While she survived,
The widow entered his tomb, having put the idea firmly into her head
That she wished to accompany him on his journey to the kingdom of
    the dead.
Behold what results when friendship is conducted in this excessive
    fashion –
It renders the sufferer conclusively impervious
To reason! A slavegirl chose to follow her mistress hither out of
    compassion,
Resolved to remain with her, expiring in her servious.
Resolved, let us be clear, without having given the proposal more than
    a cursory
Inspection, and yet ready and willing to see it through.
The lady and the slavegirl had shared a common nursery,
That is, been put to the same wet-nurse, and it is true
To say that each doted on the other
And, with the passing of the years, were only the more inclined each
    one to smother
Her companion in affection. The reader can have no notion
Of the extent of the slave's and mistress's mutual devotion.
Now this juncture found the slavegirl revealing
More solid sense than the lady, and she refused to be borne off on the
    first flood of tender feeling,
And it was the social inferior
Who tried (albeit in vain) to recall her mistress to the normally
    accepted criteria.
The widow, however, was inaccessible to every consolation
And strove by all possible means to follow the deceased on his
    Stygean peregrination:
Steel would of course have been the best and the most expeditious,
But the lady was determined to feast her eyes on her beloved and
    see 'im
In continuity as he lay within his bier; no other nourishment could be
    half so nutritious
As that of which she might partake in her late spouse's mausoleum.

Of all the exits available, the one chosen by the widow was that of
     inanition:
Day followed day without her accepting any morsel of nutrition
Other than useless sighs and tears, a litany of stark recrimination
Against the gods, the fates, indeed the entire creation.
In fact her sorrow, as it was plain to see,
Was all-embracing: it dotted every i, crossed every t.

Not far from this tomb, Death offered a rather different exhibit:
Another corpse subsisted
Whose monument consisted
Of nothing other than a highwayman's unsightly gibbet –
He had been left there to dangle
So that other robbers might see their prospective futures from an
     interesting angle.
Here a sentinel, subject to a handsome remuneration,
Kept his vigilant station.
And in the appropriate ordinance there was made mention
That, should any brigand, friend or kinsman come to purloin the
     corpse and be afforded scope
To do so by the soldier's inattention,
The said soldier would take the corpse's place at the end of the rope.
Such a sentence was undoubtedly too hard,
But the public weal refused the smallest mercy to the guard.
Through the fissures of the tomb he noticed, come the night,
A sort of radiance emanating, a most unusual sight,
And, spurred by curiosity,
He made his way thither with considerable velocity.
As he drew near,
The sound of the lady's grieving assailed his ear,
So in he went, and in much perplexity requested of her an explanation
For those tears, that doleful dirge, that dark and thoroughly lugubrious
     habitation.
Preoccupied as she was, though, with her keening,
The widow scarcely heard his shallow questions or hoisted in their
     meaning.

It was the dead man who answered for her without recourse to words, giving
The reason why the lady in her misfortune was thus entombed even while yet living.
"Having sworn our oath," the slavegirl said, "we would as lief
Permit ourselves to die of hunger and of grief."
Now although this sentry had clearly never enrolled
In a school of oratory, he nonetheless made present to them all that life could hold.
This time the widow gave the soldier renewed
Attention, and the erstwhile passion was in consequence subdued.
Time takes a hand. "If honouring your oath forbids you to eat," the man pursued,
"Why not just watch me dining? – that won't keep you clear of Hades."
A temper of his sort was not displeasing to our two young ladies,
And therefore he obtained their authorisation
To go away and fetch his evening collation,
Which he did, while the slavegirl began to detect in herself a certain ambiguity
Of sentiment as regards keeping the dead man company in perpetuity.
"A thought, dear Madam," she said, "has only now assailed
My mind: what difference does it make to your spouse if your life be thus curtailed?
Is it your opinion that he would be the man to behave
In similar fashion, had you instead preceded him into the grave?
No, Ma'am. What may be said with utter surety
Is that he would have lived his life until its full maturity.
We too may look forward still to years a-plenty
If we desist from our proposal to enter our biers at the tender age of twenty.
We'll have all the leisure to take up residence in this charnel house at a future date;
Death tends to come too early. No one's pressing. Let us wait.
As for me, I'd as soon postpone the Reaper's embrace
Until I have sufficient wrinkles on my face.

83

Is it really your wish to carry your beauty to the grave? Has it not
    entered your head
That there is but little virtue in being ogled by the dead?
Time was, as I beheld these treasures wherewith the heavens have seen
    fit to adorn you,
I'd say, 'Alas, the day will come when we must bury all these your
    charms, and mourn you!' "
At this flattering discourse the lady roused herself from her mortal
    slumber.
The god who instils love bided his time, then drew arrows, two in
    number,
From his quiver. Once these were despatched,
The first one pierced the soldier to the quick, the second left the widow
    somewhat scratched.
Youthful she was and comely, and beneath her tears resided an
    effulgent splendour.
Indeed, persons of discerning taste might well have been more than
    fond
Of her – even those persons bound to her in the nuptial bond.
The guard adored the lady: her tears, his compassion were bound to
    lend 'er
A charm of that special kind that Love assorts: the observation is well
    founded
That beauty allied to tears is beauty that's compounded.
Behold therefore the lady giving ear to one who wheedles and flatters –
See Love's first draught of poison, that leaves a person's resolutions all
    in tatters.
Behold our widow partaking of a little nourishment,
For she is not indifferent to the man who is the source of this
    encourishment.
He did all that needed doing in order to capture her affection
And made himself more deserving of her love than the handsomest
    corpse that had ever undergone the lady's inspection.
In fact the result of his achievement
Was to give her a new attitude towards bereavement;
He did this, as you may imagine, only by degrees,
Drawing her along from step to step in his constant effort to please.

I confess that I find in this no reason for surprise.
She paid attention to her persuasive swain
And as a result was soon a married woman again –
All under her late lamented husband's eyes.

With the wedding thus in progress, a robber had the temerity
To remove that for whose custody the guard had been selected.
The guard therefore, hearing the noise, ran thither with the maximum
    celerity
But all in vain – the dangling corpse, it seems, had been collected.
He returned then to the tomb in order to give the ladies an
    explanation
Of his difficulty, quite at a loss as to how he might retrieve the
    situation.
Seeing the poor fellow quite at his wits' end,
Here is what the slavegirl said unto their hapless friend:
"So your hanged man's been purloined. This is of course an
    inconvenience,
The more so if, as you say, the Law will treat you without lenience.
Well, if Madam is willing, I have the obvious solution:
We shall put our own corpse there by way of substitution.
Nobody who passes
Will notice the difference, not even if they're wearing glasses."
The lady gave her leave, deciding that this was suitable.
O Woman: you will forever be flighty and rather mutable!
You will forever be . . . woman. Some of your number are possessed
Of beauty, while others of you, I fear, are not so blessed.
Were loyalty to be the virtue that you held most dear,
You'd every one of you have your attractions, and to spare.

Prudes, be wary of your strength, and take care not to boast.
If your goal is to resist seizing the bait,
Allow me to indicate
That ours is a good one too, indeed better than most.
It is only when we try bringing it about
That you and we are equally put out.

Witness our widow. And, *pace* the good Petronius, the event (be it said
    without asperity)
Was not so wondrous as to be proposed for an example to posterity.
If the lady offended, where lay the damage, in your estimation?
Nowhere but to the rumour whereon was built her reputation,
Nowhere but to the plan pursued by the bereaved
To end her life – a plan as ill-designed as it was misconceived.
After all, to take her late lamented's corpse and string it up with
    a noose
Is surely not an action that finds no excuse,
The more so in its consequence that her new lover was reprieved.
All things considered, one is entitled to presume
That a helot on his feet has greater value than a Caesar in his tomb.